Amidst
The Tides Lies
A Beautiful
Island

Amidst
The Tides Lies
A Beautiful
Island

MANGALA

PARTRIDGE
A Penguin Company

Partridge books may be ordered through booksellers or by contacting:

Partridge India
Penguin Books India Pvt.Ltd
11, Community Centre, Panchsheel Park, New Delhi 110017
India
www.partridgepublishing.com
Phone: 000.800.10062.62

CONTENTS

FOREWORD

Writing a book needs more than just grammar and vocabulary. An inspiration at the root and reflection at every level are the basic ingredients. In this money-crazed world where every second is counted in terms of how much more one could earn, only a few can soar over such materialism. Mangala is one of them. Today, after so much experience in blogging she still writes for the pure joy of it. Reading her book I realized how many things have played on her mind—childhood memories, a soulful relationship with simple things, marvelling at the glory of nature and all those small thoughts and feelings we usually push to the back of our minds. It is wonderful that one can string all of those together into a beautiful story, a story that describes the journey into a young girl's heart.

Neha Xavier

Channel manager, Sulekha.com.

Writer by profession.

This is my maiden attempt in writing a story. I dedicate this to the two important men in my life. I thank my father who became my fan after reading my blogs in Sulekha. He wanted me to come up with a book which I felt wasn't my cup of tea. I attempted this book as my gift to him on his 83rd birthday.

Thanks are due to my husband who supported me and inspired me to write when I decided to quit. He had no choice but to read my script for which I owe extra thanks.

Thanks to my darling daughter, Sounderya, who gave me the photo for the cover of my book even before I started jotting and to my sweet nieces, Kavya and Divya. To Kavya—whose sketch inspired this story and to Divya—who gave a finishing touch to my story with her beautiful sketch.

Change is the order of life they said

Change is the essence of life too

By choice, forced or by chance,

To suit all the roles I did transform,

Only to find myself lost midway

When will I find myself? Oh God!

TIDE 1

All along we walked together,
In joy and sorrow, in ups and downs
You held me, wiped my hurt,
When the world turned me down
Ma, you are God in human attire.

She finished cooking and cleaned the kitchen. There was pin drop silence in the house. She could hear the music that came wafting in the air. It had been playing invading everyone's peace for almost a week. She came to know from her maid that it was for a temple festival. She was against this sound pollution, but there are many who loved this loud speaker culture. They want to announce each and everything. It is nothing but display of wealth and power. The philosophy is very simple. God never wants any pomp or show. But people need to do these to show others that they are more devoted than others. It is a way adopted to satisfy one's ego. At some point of time in our life, we are compelled to go with the crowd whether we like it or not. We give an attractive title to it as "social compulsion". One who does not want to be a part of the crowd is cursed as a sociopath. She took a deep breath and smiled to herself. Isn't life that way? You are compelled to do many things you don't approve of and hate.

She took the book she was reading, "Literature and Life" and walked to her favourite spot in the dining room.

She relaxed in the chair near the window. The window had been the world to her, when she was a kid. With her mother by her side, feeding her with stories and food, she enjoyed the parrots, the mynahs, the crows that came to have a taste of her food. As she grew up, the way she saw things too changed. The beauty of nature unfolded the wings before her eyes. She sat with her mother together reading, appreciating, criticising and enjoying poetry, novels, classics, modern, anything under the sun. Her mother was very conversant with Sanskrit, English and Tamil poems, poets and authors whereas she had only limited knowledge in Sanskrit and Tamil.

The world outside the window has lots to say and show. One has to listen in silence and with interest. The landscape is the same but the themes differ. No matter how many times, how many days or years, nature has a wonderful way of captivating ones heart, be it the dry leaf shedding autumn or scorching summer or rainy season. The chair took the position near the window, when they moved to this house. It had the luxury of watching everything inside and outside the window. It was a lucky soul, she thought. She smiled patting on its arms gently. Does lifeless mean no soul? But all the happiness and sorrow of hers and her family was a part of that chair too. That's how she thought of it. She loved the chair right from her birth. She couldn't think of it as lifeless. It was also a part of her, like her mother and sister.

She tried concentrating on the book. She had a lecture to be given to her class after a week. But her mind wasn't calm; it was drowned in worries and sorrows that reading a page took her almost an hour. Her eyes went absently outside the window. It was dark and gloomy, with the balance of the stopped rain still dripping. It dripped one, two and three, drop by drop from the neem leaves to a small hibiscus plant and a jasmine creeper under it. The hibiscus flower, all wet and shivering, held the drops that fell, swaying gently, trying to hold the pearls in her beautiful red bowl. After some time, it couldn't bear the weight and slowly swayed to a side pouring out the water, just like a charitable person, who gives away his accumulated wealth to all poor and needy. The flower again stood straight ready, to save the pearls for charity. The water, dropped by the flower, fell on the ground and some into the mud pot which housed croutons with large pink flowers and a big bull frog and small frogs. It was funny to hear them sing in chorus whenever they were bathed. Nature looked very beautiful even in this gloomy dark moment.

Her eyes again went up to the neem tree and there sat a small, very small yellow bird with a brown coat and a red mouth. She was all wet. She tried to keep herself warm by making herself fluffy. She looked funnily fat and her eyes were closed, as if she was meditating. With every wind, the tree and leaves swayed, her tail shivered, leaves showered more droplets on her as if it wasn't satisfied with her cleanliness. She quivered, fluttered her wings and slanted her head and went back to reverie. She looked lonely; maybe she too was like her, all alone in this wide, vast world even with millions and trillions of lives around. As if sensing her thoughts, the little brown coat opened her eyes and started seeing towards her. She remembered Frost's lines in "The Tuft of Flowers" about being alone

And I must be, as he had been-alone
As all must be, 'I said within my heart,
Whether they work together or alone'.

She saw the birdie and the birdie eyed her with curiosity. May be the birdie thought herself lucky, as she was free and sky was her limit. Megha was behind an enclosure. She was trapped, unable to free herself from the criticism of the society, from the worldly things, a prisoner of desire and worldly pleasures. She remembered reading somewhere that body is a house and soul is imprisoned in it. Once we renounce everything, we get to know the self, the soul and can experience extreme happiness. As if to agree with her mind's rambles, little brownie nodded her head, fluttered her wings and turned a wee bit to get a full view of her. Telepathy—though she wasn't sure if such things existed, she was forced to believe, when her mother read her thoughts. Now it was the birdie and Megha. Megha's thoughts to the birdie and the birdie's thoughts to Megha, exchange of thoughts via mind not via words. How beautiful it is. Nature is kind, very generous, never like the people around.

Megha, her mother was very proud of giving her that name. She loved Kalidasa's works. It seems she was reading "Meghadoota", when she got her labour pains and decided then and there to name her daughter Megha. The people around her considered it apt, when they saw the black, dense hair that curled and fell on the baby's forehead which resembled dark cloudsEven now, she is envied for her long black dense hair. Her mother was a soft, kind and generous person. But, when it came to principles, she never compromised. Seeing her and following her footsteps, Megha too was like her. Her mother was the only one who stood for her, supported her and still lives for her. A cough from the bedroom brought her back to earth. She took the porridge she had prepared and ran to her mother.

TIDE 2

In tears, I stood,
Waiting for you to wipe
The hand that wiped
My fears and tears
Now stare alien at me

Megha entered the room with a bowl of porridge in her hands. She felt sad to see her mom's plight. It is more than a month, since her mom fell into this state of shock. She couldn't recognise anyone, even herself. The doctor had asked Megha to keep talking and interacting with her mom which they felt may bring a change in her. So, it had become a routine to talk to her mom, while feeding and while going to bed. She had the whole Sunday to herself, when she read out books her mom admired, to her. Each night passed with a hope that the morning will bring a change in her mom.

After Megha gave a few spoonfuls of porridge, her mom refused to eat. Megha placed the bowl on the table and started talking to her mom. "Amma, I am Megha. Do you remember why you gave me this name. You told me that I got the name from Meghadoot of Kalidasa. Will you recite me again, the lines you loved, Ma? When will you start talking to me? Do you know that I am confused, want to ask you many things and am waiting for you to talk and recognise me. Shall I tell you the lines from Meghadoot? Will you eat then? You need to eat to become strong."

Megha recited her mom's favourite lines from Meghadoot, the ones her mother always cherished. The doctor had told her that reminding her of the old moments and the things she loved might bring back her lost memory. Her mother usually recited in Sanskrit and then gave her the English translation after that. Megha knew only the English version. Having heard from her mom, right from the age of four, she remembered the lines by heart. "Meghadoot' means 'cloud messenger'. These lines were told by a yakshan who was imprisoned by a king. He remembered his wife and sent a message through the clouds (megha). These lines were written, when the yakshan tells the messenger about how to reach his country to deliver the message to his wife

> *And when they hear thy welcome thunders break,*
> *When mushrooms sprout to greet thy fertile weeks,*
> *The swans who long for the Himalayan lake*
> *Will be thy comrades to Kailasa's peaks,*
> *With juicy bits of lotus-fibre in their beaks*
> *One last embrace upon this mount best*
> *Whose flanks were pressed by Rama's holy feet,*
> *Who yearly strives his love for thee to show,*
> *Warmly his well-beloved friend to greet*
> *With the tear of welcome shed when two long-parted meet.*

Megha's mom was well known for her oratory skills. Her lectures had earned her a lot of fans. According to her mom, any work, whatever it is, should be done with dedication and love. She believed that when a job is done with joy, we will start enjoying and appreciating, even the ones we feel are uninteresting or drab. Once we start enjoying, we will fall in love with the subject or work. She practised whatever she preached.

Whenever her mother recited her favourite lines to Megha, her eyes danced, as if she was viewing the Himalayas, the Kailas peaks, the swans and the lotus flowers. Even the audience experienced that ecstasy, when words danced on her tongue. She explained each and every word enjoying to the depth and living every single expression. She had a taste for poetry, be it English, Sanskrit or Tamil. Megha was happy that she could appreciate poetry. That way she felt herself being too close to her mother than her sister Bharathi, who was interested in finance and business

According to her sister, literature was a waste. It surely cannot buy a man a house or food. She always teased her mom that poets were either insane or poor and that's the only thing literature can do. Her mother replied that it brought joy and happiness. Her sister said that money can do more. She calculated everything in terms of money.

Megha saw a glint of delight and recognition in her moms' eyes, when the words from the poems were spelt out. She slowly held her mother's hands and started feeding her again. She never thought that this could happen to her mother. Her mother had fed her, when she was young, along with moral stories and puranas. She never dreamt that her mother would come to this stage and she would have to feed her.

Megha started telling her, "Do you remember your friend, Swathi Ma, she called today to know how you are doing. She wanted to know if she can be of some help. Ma, its dark today. Its raining So I did not fill the water bowl for the birds. I plucked a few flowers for pooja and came back home."

On Sundays, she managed everything on her own. She gave a break to Muthu who took care of her mom on weekdays. Muthu is a very sincere and loyal woman who helped her mom out in domestic jobs and gave her moral support too. She had been there with them from the time she remembered. So Megha felt it is an insult to her, if she referred to her as domestic help. She called her Muthu amma, as she was like a mother to her. So it will be a sin to call her a maid.

Megha's mom looked keenly at her face, when Megha spoke. She watched her face and lips, also when Megha read out to her. She refused to eat after sometime. Megha gave her some water and the tablets. She slept immediately and slipped into her world. Megha couldn't tell, if she had any thoughts going on in her mind. Megha brushed the hair that fell on her mom's face and slowly wiped the water around her lips.

Megha watched her mom with tears in her eyes. It was painful to see her mom in this state, this active lady who dominated every action in the house, staying still. It was in just a moment, a flash of a second that everything happened and the whole world had come to a stand still for her mom and her. All because of that wicked, cruel hearted man called her father. He had not only damaged the relationship between them but also planted hatred in her towards all men in the world.

It was really surprising that a strong lady like her mom can fall prey to the cruel words of her husband; their father. She did not feel like eating her lunch or read anything. She sat by the window with the gloom filled heart brooding about the things that had happened. She thought of the doctor who treated her mom and who visited them to check on her on Sundays. Her mind raced back to the moment her father entered the life upsetting the smooth flow of the stream.

TIDE 3

We dream and make plans
We desire things to happen
With a click of our fingers
And at the wink of our eyes
Little knowing we aren't masters
For the next step or moment

Megha sat brooding about the fateful day, when her mom was pushed into this condition. She remembered everything clearly. They were both in the kitchen discussing about the admission process in the college. Megha told her mom, "There aren't much takers for arts. Only students who fail to get admission in any other course choose arts, Amma, people don't realise that language, literature and history are also essential in life." Megha's mom too agreed.

Mom said, "No one likes to take Sanskrit, as you cannot earn a large sum of money by teaching it. Only people who really love that language come to learn it. Megha, I was surprised to see a woman aged fifty in my class. She told me that it was her dream to learn Sanskrit and read all the works of Adi Shankara. She had waited for her daughter and son to finish their education and get settled. Now that she was free, she had enrolled. I feel proud of her. Many students from Europe and America enrol to learn the history of this language. It was surprising to see them do research on the languages that stemmed from Sanskrit and the words that had got mixed with other languages. Do you know Megha, there is a village in Karnataka, in South India called Mattur, where people use Sanskrit for day to day communication?"

Megha looked surprised on hearing this. She said, "How do they speak such a complicated language, ma?" Her mom laughed, "No Megha, there is no complication, when you are used to the language. Like we feel Tamil is easy as we use it from the day you were born. Take Chinese, isn't that a complicated language?. Look at the way they write. Still the kids whose mother tongue is Chinese don't find it difficult. It's only a matter of getting used to the language. Megha! I have to help some research students in the college so I need to be there today by two after lunch. We have to meet Bharathi in the hospital at five in the evening. You come to my college. Then we will both go from there together to the hospital." Megha replied, "Yes ma, I will meet you in your college at four. I wish Bharathi gets better soon, ma." Her mom took a deep breath and wished the same too.

Their talk was interrupted by continuous ringing of the door bell and a harsh knock. They both looked at each other with a puzzled look. They switched off the stove and Megha followed her mom who opened the door. She stared at the figure which stood at the entrance. Megha, with all curiousity peeped above her mom's shoulder to see the guest. She was surprised to see a shabby man staring at his mom with angry eyes. Megha couldn't understand as to why her mom did not close the door. The smell of liquor hit the air.

Megha was in for a shock, when her mom asked the man in. The man started hurling abuses at her mom. She had never in her life come across such harsh and indecent words. When he accused her of spoiling his life and his daughters', Megha understood who he was. She did not recognise her father at first, as she was only five when he left her and had not seen him thereafter. Her mom started to say something but suddenly fell onto the chair that was nearby.

The man who continued with his abuses stopped short seeing Megha. He asked, "Arent you Megha? How much you have grown? Do you know how much I miss you both? It was your mom's arrogance, pride and ego that made me stay away from you both." Megha interrupted him, "I don't know who you are and I don't like the sight of you. Will you please go out and leave us in peace?" He started saying, "Megha, listen.". But she opened the door and asked him to get out. When he started abusing his mom again, she said harshly, "Are you going out or shall I call the police Mister?" He went out saying that Megha had inherited all the bad qualities of her mother. She shut the door, as soon as he walked out being afraid that he might enter again.

She rushed to her mom, "Amma, are you alright. You shouldn't have let him in, amma. Why are you silent? What is wrong with you?" She shook her mother. But her mom looked faint and shocked. She ran into the kitchen. When she returned with a glass of water, she found that her mom's eyes were closed. She sprinkled water on her face and waited for her to open her eyes.

She opened her eyes but stared blankly and bewildered. Megha shook her and called "Amma, amma, look at me . . . ." She looked at her puzzled and asked, "Who are you?". Megha stood shocked and blown. She did not know what to do. She was jittery, nervous and scared. She called Nirmala, Muthu's daughter, a doctor. When Nirmala answered the phone, she wept, "Come soon Nirmala.

Amma is not well. I am afraid. She is unable to identify me." Nirmala asked her to be calm and said, "I will be there soon. Keep calm, Megha."

Megha sat near her mom, took her hands and asked her what had happened. That man, her father hadn't turned up all these 25 years. He had not seen his kids after the separation. Then Megha thought," why did he come all the way today?. What was the reason?.What made a strong lady like her mom sink?. Why did she allow him to enter the house?

Megha sat shocked unable to decide what she was to do. She offered her a glass of water She spoke, she pleaded, wept and cursed the demon who did this damage. But her mom did not even wink. She sat there as if she was watching someone talking. The face that always had a smile, stood ashen. Her eyes wore no expression but stood still and the mouth that voiced honey sweet words stayed silent. The fearless, bold and beautiful woman sat lost and with fear smitten in her eyes. She had started to hate her father so much that she did not want to meet him in future, even if he repented for the things he had done.

She saw the clock that was ticking away. She waited for Nirmala to come. "Will Nirmala bring back amma to normal state or is it something very serious?" Megha wondered. She wondered why the man who was believed to be a very rich man, came in dirty clothes and drunk. She took the tumbler and tried to make her drink. She again asked., "Amma, look at me . . . why don't you talk?" Seeing it was fruitless, she sat exhausted and tired with all energy drained out, staring at the clock waiting for Nirmala to come.

TIDE 4

M egha's mom continued to be in the non-responsive state. Megha kept praying God that her mom should get well soon. Nirmala was Megha's childhood friend. She had become a daughter in that household along with Megha and her sister. Nirmala came running up the stairs and rang the bell. When Megha opened the door She asked, "Where is amma? What happened to her?". Megha showed Nirmala, the state in which her mom was sitting.

Nirmala checked mom's pulse. She held the face of her mom in her hands and turned it towards her. She could see the eyes wearing a blank look. There was no sign of recognition. She called out "Vasundhara Amma", for that was how she always addressed her. But, Vasundhara looked as if the words were addressed to someone else. When Nirmala shook her, Vasundhara asked Nirmala, "Who are you?", the same question she had asked Megha. This query brought fear in the heart of Doctor Nirmala too.

Megha thought that her mom was in a state of shock, after seeing the man whom she had never expected to see. She thought she would recover after a few minutes. But the way things were going, she lost her hope. The look in Nirmala's eyes did not spell any hope to her. So Megha felt herself grow weak and nervous. Nirmala could sense tears peeping out of her eyes too for the woman who gave her a life. It is very difficult to control ones tears, when the person one adores, loves and worships, is in trouble. Nirmala gave her an injection to ease the anxiety and called for an ambulance. She called her friend, a neurosurgeon. She quickly briefed him about Vasundhara's health condition. She asked him to wait in the hospital, as she was expecting the ambulance at anytime.

While waiting for the ambulance, Megha described to Nirmala, between sobs, what had happened. Nirmala too was puzzled at the sudden appearance of Megha's dad. As far as Nirmala knew, from her mom, Muthu, the man had never visited after Vasundhara and her husband broke off. She was told that he was very rich, married, had two sons and was in Mumbai. This information had been given by a friend of Vasundhara who had met him in Mumbai some years back. Vasundhara said that she did not want to know anything about the chapter in her life that was closed and torn. The way Megha described, her dad looked funny. She wondered why a rich man should come shabbily dressed, dirty and drunk. Vasundhara was now sleeping.

Both Megha and Nirmala sat beside Vasundhara in silence. Life is full of twists and turns. When everything is smooth we seldom realise that there may be a bump or a pit at any corner or at any moment. We take life for granted. Megha couldn't believe that her mom who was talking to her normally a few minutes ago, is now devoid of any expression and sense. She started having the doubt, if she would ever see her mom back in normal condition. Nirmala, being a doctor, had heard of these conditions. But she was surprised to see a strong woman like amma being afflicted with this condition.

Nirmala wondered about what would have crossed her mind, when she met the long lost relation. Was she scared? Or was she reminded of the unpleasant past. Nirmala thought, "Brain is an organ which cannot be unfortunately expected to behave the same way for all the people. Hence it will be very difficult to analyse what causes depression in some, why emotional stress is more for some and so on. She saw the time and thought of checking with the hospital when was the ambulance sent and precisely at the same moment the door bell rang.

As Vasundhara was sleeping, she was transferred to the ambulance in a stretcher. Megha took her handbag, locked the door and ran down to the ambulance. Megha saw her mom was not moving even a limb, when she was transferred.

On the way to the hospital, Megha asked Nirmala, "What do you think has happened to ma? Why is she unable to recognise us?" Nirmala replied, "See Megha, I don't see any serious problem. You have to be calm. She will be back to normal soon. Don't worry." Megha was silent. The ambulance entered the multispeciality hospital. Nirmala got down first and asked the attenders to shift her mom into the hospital. Nirmala walked to a person who was standing in the entrance. She started telling him about Vasundhara's condition, when Megha walked towards them along with her mom in the stretcher.

The doctors asked the attenders to take the stretcher to the room which had a display "Emergency ward" on it. Nirmala introduced Megha to the person she was talking to as Dr. Subramanian. She said that he was a neurosurgeon and also her friend. Dr. Subramanian was a tall, fair person with a pleasant smile scattered all over his face. His eyes looked kind and sympathetic. He said, "Don't worry, madam. We will find out what is the problem and make her normal. That is why we are all here. Don't worry. Please be seated in that bench. We will check your mom and get back to you." Nirmala patted Megha and walked along with him to the emergency room.

A nurse came to Megha with a pen and a paper to note down details regarding the health of her mom she asked Megha, "Tell me the details of the patient, madam. What's her name and age?". Megha replied. "Vasundhara and age is 56." The nurse asked, "Diabetes, hypertension, has she got any complaints? Is she on any drugs?" Megha answered, "No, she has no complaints and she has never taken any medicines." The nurse walked back to the room. Megha felt the nurse to be robotic. She had a funny sing song intonation.

Megha had never seen her mom fall sick. Very rarely, she used to get cold and cough but she never took any medicines for it. She was a very healthy person stuck to her routine and her diet. She always got up around four in the morning before twilight. She did her yoga exercises, meditation and strolled in the garden to pluck the flowers that were bathed in dewdrops and to welcome the birds that came to have a dip in the big pot of water which she always kept in the garden.

She plucked only a few flowers for pooja and left the rest to the bees and birds. She used to eat or drink something, only after she bathed and finished her pooja. Megha had never seen her change the routine or being lazy. She was a strict disciplinarian. By the time the sisters woke up half the work would be over. From the time she remembered, Megha has always seen her mom in a crisp cotton saree whether she was at home or at work.

Megha had never seen her mom idle. If it was not kitchen work, she cleaned the house or garden or she sat down to read some book or article or newspaper. She had a wide range of interests. She also was a good singer and an admirer of Carnatic music and bhajans. She played them in the morning or night and sang along with it. Megha inherited the artistic qualities from her. It pained Megha to see her ever cheerful and enthusiastic mom sick in bed. If only she had the power to rewind time, she mused, she would erase the time her dad had come at their door to upset their life.

Megha stood staring at the closed doors praying for a miracle to happen. She was expecting to see her mom regain her consciousness and become normal, when the closed doors opened. Dr. Subramanian, came from the emergency room and told Megha, "we have put her on some medicines. I want to shift her to ICU to monitor her for a day or two. We will take the scans of brain to see, if there is any problem. If you want to see her, madam, you can see her now. Once she is inside the ICU, you won't be permitted in."

Megha asked him, "What do you think about my mother's recovery doctor? Will my mom get well soon? She was completely normal in the morning. There was not even a sign of discomfort in her. She was happy and healthy." The doctor thought for a while, then said, "I heard from Nirmala that she went into this condition after seeing your dad. May be she was shocked to see him enter her life again or may be something he uttered affected her or scared her. Don't worry, madam, we will find out what the problem is and then decide what treatment to be given. I will see you after the scans are taken and we get the results."

Megha went into the emergency ward to see her mom. The nurses were getting her ready to shift her to ICU. They had put her on saline and Megha saw a mask on her mom's nose. She asked Nirmala about it. Nirmala replied, "Oh, it's nothing Megha, mom was having low blood pressure and her pulse was a bit weak, so that's an oxygen mask that will help her breathe easily." Megha doubted, if Nirmala was speaking the truth

Megha watched her mom being wheeled into the ICU. She wanted to hold her mom's hands for a moment. She felt she would need some courage to tackle the present situation. So she held her mom's hand before the stretcher could enter the ICU. The nurse gave a sympathetic look and stayed out a few minutes before entering. Nirmala hugged her and said, "Megha, I will be there with mom. I obtained permission from the doctor. So don't worry. Be strong. Go home Megha. I will stay with mom. You can come in the morning. She is not in any danger. Believe me Megha."

Megha shook her head," No, Nirmala, I am not going anywhere. I will wait outside the ICU. I think, I can sit here. What am I going to do at home?. I don't want to leave mom and go. "Nirmala told her," The time is four now and you haven't had your lunch yet. Go to the canteen, Megha and have something to eat. You can sit in the visitors' room after taking something. I will call you, if I need anything."

Megha replied, "Nirmala I am not hungry. I am only worried about mom. I am afraid that she will leave me alone in this vast world. I will take something, if I am hungry. Where is the room for the visitors? Dont worry about me Nirmala. I will be fine."

Nirmala told Megha, "If you don't eat, you won't be strong enough to handle things. You go straight and the turn right, the vistors' room is on the right side corner. "Megha nodded faintly and walked towards the visitors' room. Nirmala watched Megha walk slowly and then entered the ICU. Megha found the room and opened the door, when the speaker above the door was calling someone called Prem in that room to go to the doctors' room.

Nirmala asked a nurse, who was going out, to buy something for Megha to eat. She knew that Megha would not go by herself and eat. She saw Vasundhara was still in deep slumber. She saw the face that looked beautiful and speckless reflecting her heart that was pure and generous. Vasundhara Amma was more than her mother to Nirmala, her Goddess who helped her to accomplish her dreams.

Nirmala had aspired to be a doctor from her childhood days, but it was possible only with Vasundhara's help. If not for Vasundhara, Nirmala thought, her mom would have got her married to a drunkard and she would have been a mother by now. Muthu, her mom, wanted to kill Nirmala as soon as she came to know that the child was a girl. Female infanticide was quite common among the village folks. They did not feel guilty about it. Whenever Nirmala came across poems or lessons on mother's love, she laughed at it saying it as tall claims. She had never seen a mother in her village who showered unconditional love towards their children.

The way these mothers killed the new born was very cruel. Either they add a grain of rice to milk and feed the baby or use erukkam (Calotropis Gigantica) milk that kills the kid due to the poisonous quality in it. She also would have ended up in the grave, if her aunt who had come to visit Muthu, told her to keep the child so that she can help her out in household work and for babysitting the babies she was to have in future. Her aunt, a very strategic woman, asked her mom to do away with the girls, if they are born after Nirmala. Nirmala came to know about this from her mom who is now campaigning against female infanticide. Thanks to Vasundhara Amma who made Muthu realise the worth of a daughter.

Vasundhara respected everyone. She gave a lot of confidence and moral support to Nirmala. Many times, during her schooling, she had lost her confidence in studies and even decided to give up her education. But, Vasundhara used to tell her stories on the lives of many famous people who had struggled early in their life to reach the place. She always felt rejuvenated after talking to Vasundhara amma. Amma was straight forward, honest and selfless.

Nirmala was still confounded that Amma's husband could harbour so much hatred towards such a kind hearted lady. Isn't it true that a diamond is precious to a person who knows the value of it or else it is just a white stone.

TIDE 5

Nirmala watched her mentor rest as if her body had decided to take a break from the cluttering and struggles faced by her in life. Vasundhara always quoted a famous saying whenever Nirmala grumbled of any stumbling block that "Oaks grow strong as they stand the contrary winds and diamonds are made under pressure." She always said, "You can never shine if you prefer to get things easily and want to escape instead of facing problems."

Nirmala never felt the need to visit a temple, as she saw Vasundhara as her goddess and amma's house her temple. God knows what his children deserve and gives them without being asked. Vasundhara too never waited for Nirmala to ask for anything. She knew what Nirmala needed and surprised her.

When her mom, Muthu, called her an atheist for refusing to visit the temple festival, Nirmala tried explaining her mom that she had her exams. Muthu complained about this to Vasundhara, when Nirmala visited their house after the exams, Vasundhara sweetly asked Nirmala not to disobey her elders and told Muthu that she should also understand her daughter's problems. If there was no exam, then Nirmala would have come with her to temple. Muthu passed the same comment, she usually passed," What? Is my daughter going to become a collector or minister? What education? She has to cook and take care of a kid which is the job of a woman. For that you don't need schooling."

Muthu couldn't object to Nirmala's education, as Vasundhara funded it. She couldn't find fault with Nirmala as she did all the house work giving no room for her mother to grumble. Nirmala wasn't an atheist as her mom thought. She was a believer except that her principles and ideals were different from those of others. According to her, God never demanded anything from the devotees. She did not want her mom to waste the little money she had earned through her hard labour on buying things for God to perform pooja instead of feeding her hungry brothers. She tried explaining her mom that God did not expect any offering, but wanted people to perform their duties and have a pure heart. Muthu cursed Nirmala for talking blasphemy.

People who knew Vasundhara loved her nature. Nirmala had never seen Vasundhara, angry or being impatient. She could bring sense to a person without being harsh. Her mom had told Nirmala that Vasundhara had decided to get separated from her husband, only after she couldn't take his tortures anymore. This man, who had left her 25 years ago, had come all the way to stab her on the wounds that were healing. Nirmala did not understand the logic behind her troubles and the karma theory about which Vasundhara often talked. Vasundhara never stopped helping a person in distress, though she had lot of problems herself. She never blamed anyone or showed her distress to anyone. No one would have known her real problems except for her daughters, Muthu and herself. She always believed that God knew what she deserved and gave it as and when the time was apt. Nirmala was convinced that she was destined to become a doctor. So she believed that she was made to visit Megha's house on the day, when luck brought her before Vasundhara amma. She was in the fifth standard then, when her mom had asked her to discontinue her studies. She had not gone to school for almost three months.

Muthu asked Nirmala to bring her younger brother to Megha's house, where she was a domestic help. Her brother had to be vaccinated. Muthu said that she would finish her work by then and they could take the boy to the heath center for vaccination. Nirmala came before Muthu could complete her work. So Muthu asked Megha to be with the kid in the front room. Nirmala looked at the book shelf which had rows and rows of books. She went near it and watched in admiration. Then she saw a book on a small table near the sofa. She touched it first, and then slowly turned the pages. It had Megha's name on it. Nirmala was so enthusiastic that she started reading the book aloud. She was so immersed in it that she did not notice Megha's mom watching her.

Vasundhara sat near Nirmala and watched her reading the English text book of Megha. She asked Nirmala, if she understood the meaning of what she read. She was so happy to hear Nirmala explain beautifully. When she asked her the class she was in, Nirmala started sobbing. She told her that she wasn't going to school. Vasundhara called Muthu and asked her why she had discontinued Nirmala's schooling. Muthu said that education wasn't essential for a girl and she needed the helping hands at home to look after her kids.

Vasundhara told Muthu that she would take care of Nirmala's education and she could bring her little son along with her, when she came to work in their house. Muthu couldn't do much, though she grumbled and argued with Vasundhara at first. Vasundhara kept her promise and got Nirmala readmitted in the school. It wasn't difficult as the teachers knew Nirmala's interest and intelligence. Vasundhara supported throughout her studies.

In her twelfth standard, when Nirmala heard the news that she had topped all the schools and came first in the state, she did not go to her mother, but came running to Vasundhara. Vasundhara hugged and kissed her. Nirmala also remembered Megha jumping with joy. Megha was very happy for Nirmala. She was never jealous. Megha was just like her mother. Megha scored 90% and opted for English literature, while Nirmala wanted to do medicine. Vasundhara was ready to support Nirmala, but Nirmala's mother was against it. She wanted to stop her education and get her married. She said that it would be difficult to get a groom, if she got educated further. But Vasundhara stopped her nonsense by saying that the CM of Tamil Nadu was giving an award to Nirmala after a week and also that the Government would sponsor her education, as she had come first in the state. She was the first graduate in her house too. She told Muthu that she could be photographed along with the CM whom she admired a lot. The chance of getting snapped with the CM made her immensely happy. So Muthu started waiting eagerly for that moment of bliss.

Nirmala wanted Vasundhara to be present near her, when she received the award. But Vasundhara took a back seat saying that her success was due to the effort Nirmala had put forth and she had nothing to do with it. Nirmala secured admission in the Government Medical College in Chennai. She also could get posted in that college hospital itself due to her hard work and good score. Her mother has now stopped talking anything against Nirmala after she took up the profession. She was now the root of the family, the money giver of the family.

People arealways ready to share and celebrate happiness, but there is none when difficulties surface. That is the way of the world. The mother who wanted to kill her as soon as she was born because she was a girl, the mother who did not want to educate her, the mother who did not bother about her feelings and hunger, now celebrates her and goes around places boasting that her daughter is a doctor. This woman who breathed life into her, who stood beside her whenever she felt depressed, always stood a silent spectator never boasting about what she had done to her.

Vasundhara wanted Nirmala to do PG but Nirmala said she had to help her brothers complete their education. Nirmala only had brothers. Thank God there was no girl after her whom her mother would have certainly harassed. She decided that she would pursue her higher studies only after her two brothers were settled in life. Vasundhara appreciated her and said that medical profession is a noble one. She wanted Nirmala to do full justice to it.

This angel, her guide, will she talk to her again? Nirmala held Vasundhara's hand and wept. So what, if she was a doctor? Wasn't she a human being first? What could she do, when her Goddess is not speaking? Her doubt was, whether she had a brain stroke or was she in just a state of shock. The scans taken should provide the answers. She held Vasundhara's hands and said," No amma ; you are not quitting. You need to fight and get well soon. There are many people who are waiting for your helping hands." She had to go to her hospital at nine for her night shift. She thought of asking her friend to do night duty in her place. But seeing that there was nothing she could do then and as Megha had refused to go home, she thought she would go to work so as to stay with Megha in the morning. The results of the scans will be known then.

TIDE 6

Megha felt very down, depressed, nervous and was afraid, when she left her mom in ICU and walked to the visitors' room. She saw the room on the right side of the long corridor. The reception was a few steps away from the room. She opened the door of the visitors' room which had all the chairs occupied except a few in the farther end. She walked carefully taking care not to stamp on anyone who had their legs stretched and reached the chair that was near an elderly man reading some religious book. He lifted his eyes to see her and then turned his attention to the book. There was a kid with his mom who was refusing to eat and the mom was showing him some pictures from a picture book she had with her. The mom lifted her head, saw Megha and smiled faintly.

Megha sat down and gazed around the room. The announcement system went on and called Mr. Prem to meet the doctor. There was a hustle in the front row and the man called Prem walked out of the room. The room was air conditioned and lights were on though it was only half past five in the evening. The thick dark curtains and the closed windows did not allow light to peep in. Her eyes inspected the people there. They were either reading newspapers or books or chanting something with their eyes closed. The people were mostly the relatives of the patients in ICU. So everyone was in their own world tense and sad.

The kid who was taking food now asked in its gibberish voice," Where is dad? I want to play with him." The mother made the kid sit on her lap and replied, "If you eat the food properly, then I will take you to dad. You can play with him, if you are good. The kid ate a morsel from what she gave and again asked the same question to which his mom answered patiently. Then he said," Let us go home. I want my toys and books." Megha saw the mom and kid communicating feeling sad for them both.

A nurse who entered the room was looking for Megha and gave her a small parcel and a cup of coffee. Megha thanked her. She opened the packet and saw two iddlies in it. She took a piece from it and put in her mouth. She could not swallow it. She did not feel like eating. She threw it in the trash box and drank the coffee. The mom who sat near saw her and advised," Madam, "you should be healthy to attend to the person who is in the hospital, so eat properly. Who will take care of the sick person, if you fall sick?" Megha started to weep again and the mom of the kid did not ask her anything, but just patted her on her back and said "every problem has a solution and yours too will have a solution, don't worry". Megha wiped her eyes. The kid who saw Megha weep asked his mom in his sweet voice," Why is aunty crying? Shall we give her my ball? Both Megha and the mother smiled at his innocence.

Megha turned towards the window hiding her tears from the kid. There was a poster which demanded silence with Shhhh from an image of a small girl with her golden hair let loose and a few wordings which was apt for the people there were written on it . . .

Life is merely froth and bubbles
Only two things stand like stones
Patience in others troubles
And courage in your own

When she read the lines, she knew how difficult it is to have courage when in trouble. She is experiencing it now. The fear of losing her mom stood in the back of her mind tormenting her. She saw a big clock ticking busily. The time was half past six. Time seemed to march past without any news of improvement from her mother. She had expected her mom to get better in a few minutes, then in an hour, but the hour has become hours; it was four hours since her mom fell into this condition and she was yet to recover.

Megha closed her eyes and stretched her legs. She tried to remain calm. First the scene of her mom sleeping in the ICU flashed before her eyes and then her dad's visit. That was the first time, she was seeing him after he had deserted them. She couldn't recognise him at all. The words he spoke kept running in her mind. A day started happily but ended in a dull, cruel way. That reminded her of their proposed visit to see her sister Bharathi. In this din, she had completely forgotten about her. Poor Bharathi, she would have got disappointed on not seeing them.

She went to the reception desk that was a few steps away and asked them permission to make a call. She called the operator of Ashraya, the hospital in which Bharathi was admitted and asked for Dr. Shivashankar, the doctor who was treating her. There was a short wait and a click. Then the phone started ringing. The doctor answered the call.

Megha told him, "Doctor, I am Megha, Bharathi's sister. We were supposed to meet you today. But we couldn't. My mother suddenly had an attack and she couldn't recognise anyone including herself. We have admitted her in the hospital. So we couldn't make it. I am sorry that I forgot to tell you because of the confusion and frustration here. I am really sorry Doctor." Megha paused.

The doctor replied, "It is alright. How is your mother now?". Megha replied," She is in the ICU. The doctor is saying that they will know the exact condition once the scans are taken. How is Bharathi? Was she disappointed?"

The doctor replied, "Don't worry, we did not tell her about your visit. She is doing very well. Take care of your mom. If possible, can you please come to see me around four in the evening tomorrow? You see your mom's condition and confirm your appointment." Megha said, "Sure doctor, I will try to visit tomorrow. Thank you doctor for understanding my situation" and placed the receiver. It was always her mom who took care of everything. It dawned on Megha that she has to handle everything in the place of her mom. She felt insecurity grip her.

Megha got back to the visitors' room and went to the chair where she was earlier seated. The little boy smiled and told his mom, "Ma, aunty is back, aunty is back." Megha patted the boy's cheek and asked his name. He said that his name was Sri Hari and jumped from the chair. His mom asked him to sit still and read the book she had given him. The boy stayed still for some moment then again asked for his father. He said, "Take me to dad. I want to play with him" and started to weep. She took him out for a stroll to divert his attention. She asked Megha to take care of her file and bag.

Megha closed her eyes and started praying to God to give her patience, courage and make her mom bounce back to good health. She was chalking out a plan to enable her to meet Bharathi. The mother-son pair came inside with the son smiling and clinging to a bar of chocolate in his hand. He was so happy that he sat without giving his mom any problems. Megha looked at the clock that showed that there were just five hours for the new day to be born. The mother made the kid to sleep.

The mother had a dosa she had bought in the canteen for dinner. She offered Megha from her share but Megha refused saying that she will take later. The boy was fast asleep. She put a bed sheet on the double chair and made the kid to sleep there. She too closed her eyes sitting on the chair. An announcement came in asking for Mrs. Prasad to meet the doctor. The mother became panicky. Megha could see her nervous and frightened. She asked Megha to take care of the kid and ran to meet the doctor. The elderly man who was reading a religious book lifted his eyes from the book and watched the mother go out. The old man uttered 'poor girl' and continued reading his book.

The old man asked Megha, if she could get him some water from the shop as he cannot walk and he felt sick with his wife in critical condition. Megha agreed and asked him if he had taken his dinner and if he needed anything other than water. The old man smiled faintly and said," No, I don't want to eat. I am not feeling hungry. My son will be here after sometime. He will get me something to eat. My water bottle is empty." Megha looked at the kid who was sleeping. He said, "don't worry, I will take care of the kid. I have been here from yesterday morning. That kid's mom had been here for more than a week. Poor girl, her husband met with an accident and the doctor has given up hopes. They don't think he will survive. That girl is struggling with her kid and she has no one to help her except a friend of her husband who comes to see her in the morning.

Megha went to the canteen and bought a bottle of water and a packet of biscuits for the old man. She felt sorry for the mother and the kid. Megha prayed God that the kid should not lose his father. She knew the sadness of not having a father. She knew the troubles her mother had to bear being a single mother. She did not want that situation to happen in that mother's life who seemed to be of Megha's age. She gave the water and the biscuit packet to the elderly man who blessed her with all happiness. She sat down near the kid who was fast asleep. Megha wondered how a woman with so much stress could console her so calmly. It is in a hospital that we realise how lucky we are compared to others with extreme sorrows.

Nirmala had sent a nurse named Deepa to tell Megha that she was leaving for work and Megha can sit outside ICU where there were some chairs. When Megha got up to leave, the elderly man gave her a small 'Vishnu sahasranamam' book to read and told her," Don't worry child. Your problems will get solved soon. I will take care of the kid."

She walked to the ICU. Nirmala was waiting outside. She told Megha, "Mom is stable. Even her blood pressure is normal now. She won't wake up until morning. Don't worry. I will get back in the morning. You can call my hospital number, in case of any emergency." Megha told her, "Nirmala, we were supposed to meet Bharathi's doctor today. But we couldn't. I called him and told him the reason. He asked me if I can make it tomorrow around four in the evening. So I will go to meet him tomorrow, if everything is fine with mom and you can take care till I get back." Nirmala asked her not to worry and she would be there the whole day till Megha got back. She waved her good luck, asked her not to worry and left.

TIDE 7

What is love she asked
Love comes from heart
It is not you or me
It has no ego, no greed
It's not in taking other for granted
Or change the other, the way you want
But to accept them as they are . . . .

After Nirmala left the hospital, Megha sat in one of the few chairs that were outside the ICU. There was a young man busy writing something in a diary. Megha wanted to see her mom. But she knew it was futile to ask anyone, as they followed the visiting hours strictly. They did not allow more than one person to see the patient in the ICU and that too only once day. She saw a nurse come out of the ICU with a slip in her hand and walk towards the man who was jotting in the diary. Megha hesitated at first, but later asked the nurse about her mom. The nurse told her that her mom was sleeping. She took a signature from the person and walked away

Megha sat in a chair from where she could see the ICU door open. That way she felt she was close to her mother. Nirmala was hopeful of Vasundhara becoming normal the next day and up from sedation. Megha thought, everything in life revolved around hope, hope, hope. Her mom hoped that her marriage would be a success. She hoped they would lead an ideal life. She hoped Megha would get married and be happy. She hoped her younger daughter, Bharathi would be successful in life. But each hope she held to like petals of a flower withered one by one. But her mom was strong. She still hoped that everything would fine one day. As she always said, the fruit of hardship is always sweet. Her mother waited patiently for those sweet days to come.

Megha's mom always said that the Pandavas had to wait for many years for justice, though they followed the path of Dharma and Lord Krishna was by their side. Megha had never seen her mom breakdown except on two occasions that concerned her daughters. She bounced back to normalcy very soon. When Megha and Bharathi were in college, she had told them about what had really happened to her marriage, as she felt her daughters were mature enough then to understand her emotions. The sisters could see that she still loved their father. She started recounting from the day she met their father Vasudevan.

Megha had never seen her mom's judgement go wrong. She was a person who weighed everything before taking a decision. She always said that a decision taken in a moment of anger or in hurry or emotionally always went wrong. But she herself went wrong in choosing Vasudevan as her life partner. Just like a spider who spins a web around its prey without it not knowing its being spun until it gets suffocated and dies, her father too spun a beautiful web of silk around her mother and trapped her saying it was love, only to sting her with his words and actions after they got married.

Vasundhara did her masters in Sanskrit in Chandrasekara College which was an old college. She was working there as a lecturer and was doing her PhD. Vasundhara had beautiful oratory skill. She was invited by several institutions to give lectures and she did it happily.

She had a passion for epics, dharma, Vedas and puranas. Vasudevan happened to listen to one such lecture, while passing through the lecture hall Drawn by the beauty of the voice, he became curious to see the owner of the voice. He saw Vasundhara and instantly was drawn towards her. After that he never missed even a single lecture of Vasundhara.

Vasundhara had an astonishing talent of making her speeches interesting to any group of audience, from kids to aged, from god lovers to haters. She commanded the crowd with her honey dipped voice which sailed through the air and inebriated each and everyone who were present in the territory her voice traversed. After one such lecture, Vasudevan introduced himself to Vasundhara.

Vasudevan was a MBA degree holder and a budding businessman. He appreciated her lavishly and said that he was her fan. He attended all her lectures. Slowly they started getting together. He had no one to call his own. He studied in a home run by Ramakrishna Mission. Vasundhara, being kind hearted, saw only the good qualities in him. She admired him for his broadmindedness, sincerity and honesty in whatever he did. Vasundhara's parents too loved him and thought he was an apt match for their only daughter. Vasudevan sweet talked and won the hearts of Vasundhara and her parents. After the marriage Vasundhara saw a complex setting in the mind of her better half. He always wanted people to give him importance. That wasn't a problem as her parents always treated him with respect. Life was blissful until the birth of Megha's younger sister Bharathi and Vasundhara earned a doctoral degree.

Her speeches got her fame. Everyone identified Vasudevan as Vasundhara's husband, which hurt his ego very much. He started insulting her. He wanted her to stop giving lectures. He wanted his wife to quit her job. The reason he gave was that the house needed her full attention as Megha was nearing three and her sister Bharathi was just an year old. She became the dean of the college which brought some more fire crackers in their life. Vasundhara tried talking to him but he never was to listen. The last straw was when he started doubting his wife's friendship with a professor with whom she was working for a book on ancient customs and traditions. She tried to explain to her husband. But doubt is a poisonous ivy. Once it enters, it never leaves the person till it kills him. The poison enters into every drop of blood. It makes one suspect every small action.

Marriage is a beautiful bond where love rules. Love, here means unadulterated love. There is no room for ego, doubt, jealousy, when you think the spouse as your better half. If it is going to give room to all these things, then it is just love faked and is never true. Vasudevan wanted a famous, learned and beautiful person for wooing but not as wife. He wanted his beautiful wife to give up everything.

> *If they be two, they are two so*
> *As stiff twin compasses are two ;*
> *Thy soul, the fix'd foot, makes no show*
> *To move, but doth, if the other do.*
> *And though it in the centre sit,*
> *Yet, when the other far doth roam,*
> *It leans, and hearkens after it,*
> *And grows erect, as that comes home.*
> *Such wilt thou be to me, who must,*
> *Like the other foot, obliquely run;*
> *Thy firmness makes my circle just,*
> *And makes me end where I begun*

There cannot be any better way to express love than the above lines of John Donne. It is always true and applicable to people of all generations. There are very few people who understand, support and enjoy their better half's success. Vasundhara's life started experiencing a roller coaster ride which ended with their separation.

That's how her mother's love story started like a compass with two arms held tight, but rusted mid way bringing their marriage to an end. Vasudevan wanted his wife to quit her job. Vasundara said she won't, as this suspicion was not going to end with her quitting. She felt insulted. He threatened to leave her. She thought of her darling daughters. She did not want them to miss their father's love. She tried explaining it to him but he was not ready to accept anything. He used words that hurt her, insulted her, made her feel humiliated. She agreed to separate. She knew her daughters would understand in future the circumstances under which she had to take that decision. In the court, when the talk of alimony came, she refused to take any support from her husband. He called it arrogance, in front of the judge. She did not answer, as she thought that she would not feel compelled to explain to a person who wasn't hers any more.

Though Vasundara looked very composed outwardly, Megha knew that her mother had loved and trusted her father so much that she felt betrayed. Her father married again just after a month of their separation and never came even once to see how his daughters were doing. She remembered the way he used to shout when she was young. It is said that these cruel things make deep impressions on the hearts of young ones. Bharathi was too young to remember her father. Her sister, being young, missed her father and her mom had to lie that he was abroad till she was old enough to convey her that they weren't living together. She asked many questions and her mom was always patient.

Bharathi was a person who needed an explanation for each and everything. When she came to know the real reason behind the separation, she kissed her mom and appreciated her for her decision. She looked at her mom with pride for the way she had struggled to bring them up with so much of love. She did not speak a word about her father after that. Bharathi told Megha that she would never wish to see her father or would be able to forgive him for what he had done to their mom. Vasundhara's parents fell ill and died very soon after their separation, unable to see their virtuous daughter drowned in sorrow and distress.

Vasundhara's struggle to live and bring up her kids single handedly started. Their life style changed. They moved to a smaller house. Professors did not earn much, but it was enough to maintain her kid's education and survival. Even then she did not hesitate to help Nirmala. She did all the good things she could do, setting an example to her daughters. She harboured hard. She struggled a lot to bring up her little wonders into beautiful human beings. It's easy to grow, but to be humane is difficult. She had not amassed wealth or assets for them but she gave them a beautiful life, made them humane. She taught them to work hard, to respect others and to be humble.

Megha became a lecturer after finishing her masters in English and an M.phil, following her mom's footsteps. Her sister Bharathi did MBA and went to USA for a project. Her sister was a vibrant, confident young maiden. She did extremely well in her studies and was always the topper. She never could appreciate poetry or nature. She laughed seeing Megha and Vasundhara discuss literature. Each one of us has one's own taste and ideas about life. According to her being rich, luxurious and carefree was the mantra for a beautiful life. Her dream was to shower all the comforts on her mother who had struggled so much in life.

Bharathi returned four months back all of a sudden from USA without finishing the project and was depressed and silent. It was saddening to see a bubbly girl that way. On being questioned, she did not answer. They couldn't get an answer for the sudden change, even when they called her friends in USA with whom she had shared her apartment. The friends said that she had been very normal in the morning but they found her to be in tears and sorrow when they got back home. They did not know, when she returned home or what the matter was as she did not tell them. She had booked her ticket back to India. That was the only thing she had told them. They came to know from a common friend that Bharathi had resigned quoting that she wasn't interested in working on the project.

The friends had seen her off in the air port. That's a big drawback, when you stay away from homeland. It still was a mystery, what made Bharathi get back and what happened and what ailed her. A few days after her return she went to the extent of committing suicide. That was the time her mom broke down. She was sad for Bharathi. Vasundara had no way of helping Bharathi as she did not know what was troubling her. She tried talking to her but was always answered with silence. So she decided to take her to a psychiatrist. She was admitted in the Ashraya hospital and was being treated as an inpatient. The doctor suspected it to be some depression triggered mental state and asked them not to visit her till he called. Her mom broke down, when she left Bharathi in the hospital and Bharathi did not even speak a word to her mom even after seeing her tears which was very unusual of Bharathi.

The fateful day in which Vasundara got this attack brought happiness first, when Dr. Shivasankar informed that Bharathi had started responding to his treatment. He hoped to arrange for a visit with Bharathi that day as he wanted to study Bharathi's reaction. They couldn't make the visit with her mom down. Now she was left all alone to deal the situations. She had to meet her sister tomorrow. Megha wondered how Bharathi would react on not seeing Vasundhara and what would she ask Megha. The foremost question that echoed in her mind was how she was going to handle the situation with both of them in hospital. Megha shuddered at the very thought of the future.

TIDE 8

For the first time in her life, Megha realised that she was afraid to see the day break, the daybreak which she always loved to enjoy with the sun slowly rising up the trees and spreading his hands hugging the whole earth with his golden rays. It looked as if everything l has come to a standstill with her mom in the hospital.

A nurse came to tell her that Dr. Subramanian wanted to meet her. Megha asked the nurse the way to the doctor's room. She checked the time and it was nearing five in the morning. There was a bustle of activity everywhere with the cleaners sweeping and mopping the floors, the change of shift of nurses and the doctors checking up their patients before leaving the hospital. The doctors and nurses had also been awake along with the patients, doing their duty.

Megha walked towards the doctor's room that was in the first floor. She climbed the steps avoiding the lift. She passed three rooms before she came to the room which displayed the name of the doctor. She prayed that there shouldn't be anything seriously wrong with her mom. She knocked on the door and walked in. The doctor who was studying the test reports lifted his head from the papers, when she got in. He offered her a seat. She sat and breathed deeply praying to all Gods who appeared in her mind.

The doctor smiled and told her that the sudden shut down of brain had led to the loss of her mom's recognising ability and her failure to respond and to express herself.

It is a case of shock because of which the blood pressure shoots up or goes down resulting in such a situation. She asked him whether there was any treatment which can get her mom back to normal. He said that unfortunately there wasn't and a patient could recover in a day or two, a week or after a month or even a year or years. They would put the patient under minerals and vitamins. Talking to them may help to get them back to normal. But one cannot say exactly when the brain will recover from shock.

Megha felt the earth slip under her feet. She put her hands on her face and started weeping, realising that she was helpless. She found it so difficult to handle a single day without her mother. Dr. Subramanian waited for some time. Then he said," Madam, I have heard your mother's lectures. She had positive attitude in everything and passed it on to everyone who listened to her. I can understand your pain, but you should be strong and should face the difficulties and fight because I know that's what your mother would like you to do and she would never like her daughter being depressed and helpless. We are here to help you. Be strong."

He told her to wash her face. He took her to the canteen and ordered coffee and bread toast. She refused to eat. He said that she needed food, as he could see her famished. She ate silently. The Doctor sat opposite to her munching on his toast. She asked the doctor, "Have you come across similar cases? How long did it take the patient to recover in such cases?" He said "It all depended on the impact and how one takes it. Brain is a very complex organ. Emotions aren't same. The event that can prove fatal to some one can cause just a feeling of sadness in another. A breakup may lead to depression for some, while some can just walk over it gracefully. It all depends on the individual and how they take it. It's possible that some of your father's words had hurt her so deeply that had made her crumble. So the time factor for recovery cannot be established in these type of patients. If we sit and keep talking, unmindful of her response, it may bring back her memories, when they get related within her. Miracles do happen, and Megha for all you know, she may be back from her sleep today or tomorrow morning".

The words sowed seeds of hope into her heart that was losing all faith. He said that he would keep her mom under observation her mom for two days and Megha could take her mom back home, as there was no treatment for such cases. Both of them walked to ICU silently, while Megha's mind was reliving the words of Dr. Subramanian. He too was like her mother in explaining things in a simple way to make an ignorant person understand a topic or subject with ease. She was now confident about handling things as she believed that her mom would recover soon.

The doctor asked, "Is Nirmala coming here in the morning? Can you ask her to meet me, if she comes before nine? Megha replied," Yes doctor, Nirmala will come, as I have to go to my college and apply for leave. I also have an appointment to meet my sister who is undergoing treatment. So Nirmala will stay here the whole day until I get back". They reached the ICU. When she saw her mother, Megha did not feel the same way as she had felt when she saw her mom being static for the first time. That's what her mother always said about getting used to things in life. Everything in life is very difficult, when faced for the first time, whether it is poverty or loss or illness. But, we gradually get used to it with time.

Dr. Subramanian checked her mom's pulse and slowly tapped her feet. They saw Vasundhara respond, move her feet away from his hands. Megha watched her face with lot of expectation. Vasundhara opened her eyes. She first stared at the doctor who was standing in front of her, then turned around. Her eyes met Megha's. Megha's heart started praying to be recognised. But her mom turned her eyes around. She looked at the I.V tubes. She again stared at the doctor and then at Megha. There was no sign of recognition. Megha felt sad. Vasundhara started to get up. The doctor stopped her saying she shouldn't. She asked him, "Who are you? Where am I?" Doctor replied that he was the doctor attending to her and that she was in hospital. Doctor asked her name. She first saw the doctor, as if he was speaking Greek, then she had a bewildered look in her eyes.

Doctor and Megha could see that she did not remember her name and was thinking hard. Megha told her that she was Vasundhara. But she wasn't ready to accept. She asked the doctor who was the girl standing near him. Megha introduced herself as Vasundhara's daughter. Just at that moment Nirmala entered the room. Seeing everyone around Vasundhara, she came in asking what had happened. Vasundhara turned her eyes towards Nirmala and asked in a frightened voice who Nirmala was. She was frightened and they could see that she was nervous. So the doctor asked her to take rest. He asked Megha and Nirmala to leave the room.

Megha left the room with tears blurring her vision. She saw her mom who had stood like a mountain of strength, who had a lovely memory, who could say any passage from any poem, crumble before her. Nirmala told her, "Megha, Amma will recover with time. Let's be patient. You can go home now. I had finished all my work and can stay until you get back in the evening. I have taken a day off too, as

I know that your returning after meeting Bharathi may get delayed. Are you okay Megha? Do you want me to come with you to Bharathi's hospital." "No", Megha replied "I can manage. I will feel confident, if you are here with amma.". She told Nirmala quoting the doctor that Vasundhara could be discharged in two days. Nirmala told Megha that her mother Muthu would be there with Megha till Vasundhara got better. She felt a sign of relief, when she knew that she wasn't going to be alone in the empty house.

Muthu had stopped turning up for domestic work after she had fractured her leg three years back. But she continued to make made frequent visits to see Megha and Vasundhara. When Bharathi came home from USA with sickness, Muthu was the one who stood by them and gave courage to her mom. She told her mom that everything would be fine and that she had taken a vow to walk on fire when everything got well. For her, Vasundhara was her world, her guiding light and companion. It was soothing to mind to hear that Muthu would be there for Megha. She thanked Nirmala. Nirmala patted her.

Nirmala also said that she would be with Vasundhara, whenever she was off duty. She said that Muthu would stay with her in the night too till she got the confidence to handle the situation. She asked Megha to apply leave for just a week. Doctor Subramanian walked out of the room. He said that he had given sedation to relieve Vasundhara of her anxiety. He asked Nirmala to call him, if she saw any improvement. He discussed with her about the scan reports, what he felt about it and the medications required.

The doctor offered to drop Megha in her house on his way home. She could see that it was Nirmala's idea, as she did not want Megha to go alone and Megha's house was on the way to the doctor's house. Megha accepted the offer with initial hesitation. He said that he would be back from his rounds in an hour and they could start for home. Nirmala and Megha sat silently. There wasn't anything to speak. There was pain in both their hearts. They were sad. Nirmala held Megha's hand and squeezed it. It spoke hundreds of words. Megha leaned on to Nirmala's shoulders and wept silently.

TIDE 9

Megha left the hospital with Dr. Subramanian, after he finished his morning rounds and signed off his duty. It was around eight in the morning. The shops were closed and the pavement shop keepers were busy sweeping the places and setting up their shops. The teashops and hotels were open announcing their menu in blackboards that were kept outside the shops.

The traffic was heavy with people rushing to offices and to leave their kids in school. There were school buses and college buses piling up near the signal. She saw a puny, little girl who would be seven holding on to her brother's hand who looked like five, waiting for the signal to change. From the dress they both wore and the way they looked, it was clear that their house was invaded by poverty. It was evident that they couldn't afford a bus ride. The uniform was of a government school which was a kilometre away. She felt sad for those wee legs that would take almost an hour to reach their destination, the school.

Life catches people very young to impart the knowledge of adaptability which never comes in a child whose parents can afford comforts. Her mother always told them that adaptability was very essential in life. "Be like a willow in the wind; see how it stands because it did bend". Life is never the same. You may get to taste the fall, even when you are high up celebrating victory. It just takes a second for the entire scene to change. She had experienced it many times in her life. She took a deep breath and looked at the signal which stood red.

Dr. Subramanian broke the silence, "the traffic is always heavy during this time of the day and in the evening from five to eight". Megha replied, "I know, I always take a bus that plies this way, in the morning and evening, to and from college". When the doctor asked what she had graduated in, she replied that it was in English. He smiled, "The stars of all languages seem to reside under one roof . . . . it's interesting.".Megha reacted shyly that she wasn't a star.

The doctor asked her about her sister. She replied," Bharthi opted the road less travelled by her family . . . business and she holds a masters degree in it". The doctor asked her, "Which hospital is she in? What is her problem? When are you planning to see her today?"

She said, "I have an appointment around four in the evening. She is admitted in Ashraya for PTSD'. "Are you going alone to see your sister?", the doctor asked. She gave a sad smile, "Yes . . . I am worried how Bharathi is going to react not seeing mom".

The doctor asked her, if she could tell him, why Bharathi was admitted in the hospital. She told him everything and said that they are yet to know the reason for her sudden withdrawal. The doctor was silent for some time, when he manoeuvred his car from the traffic jam to a side road which was free from commotion.

He told her," Some end up with depression, when the people whom they had trusted most cheat. If they come to terms with the realities of life, they will slowly get out of the shell. Only people who cannot come to terms with reality stay that way forever". Dr. Subramanian turned a little towards her and smiled, while she sat listening to him.

"I have come across less pragmatic people who stick to their principles and ideals and finally break down unable to tackle with practicalities in life. There are some who want their dreams and ambitions to bloom immediately and who are unable to tackle even a small failure. A seed that is sown takes its own time to grow, flower and give fruits. One should understand that. When one fails to cope up with reality and end up going to the extent of ending their life. This happens to both kinds, people who are very successful and people who are complete failures. It is a person's attitude towards life that decides the mood".

Megha said, "Bharathi attempted suicide a week after she returned from USA. It was sheer luck that my mom had returned home, as she noticed half way to her college that she had forgotten the office keys. After taking the keys, just by chance she decided to check on Bharathi. She was completely shocked, when she saw Bharathi standing on a stool with a dupatta coiled around her neck and tied to the fan in the bedroom. She immediately got her down. Even when mom begged Bharathi to tell her what was troubling her, Bharathi continued her silence. Amma was in tears and shell shocked, as she never thought her daughter would ever come to this decision. We couldn't console her at all. Mom sat with Bharathi and tenderly asked what was worrying her. She told her sternly that death wasn't a solution to any problem. After this incidence, mom did not trust Bharathi. She did not want to leave her alone. Her hope that Bharathi would get better after a few days also waned. So she took an appointment with Dr. Shivashankar of Ashraya".

Dr.Subramanian said," Oh! ya, I have heard of him. He comes to our hospital as a visiting doctor. We call specialists when we face some problems that need their assistance."

By that time, they had reached the junction from where her house was a few steps away. She asked him to drop her in the main road and that she would walk home from there. But he took her upto the entrance of her apartment. She waved him with a thank you and saw the car disappear at the turning.

When she started climbing up the stairs, she remembered that she had not called the doctor in. She felt ashamed. Her mind was so preoccupied with thoughts that she had forgotten even the basic courtesy. She fished for the keys in her hand bag and opened the door. She felt the emptiness of the house. The vacuum was frightening. She knew that after some time, Muthu would be there to give her company. She saw the chair on which her mom sat yesterday. The tumblers were still there. She took them and went to the kitchen. The cooker was on the stove untouched. The frying pan looked confused with the half cooked veggie. Her mom's tea stood untouched. She did not feel like clearing anything. She went to the living room and sat on the chair closing her eyes with rail of thoughts flashing one by one. Tired and exhausted, she fell into a deep slumber.

She woke up to the door bells' chime. It was Muthu. She came in limping. Megha could see that Muthu was also very sad and had been weeping too. She had been in their household for a long time that every happiness and sorrow of the family was a part of hers too. This bondage is something amazing. They had no blood relationship, but the love that had grown among them was very strong and beautiful. Her dad did not come even once to see his kids or the woman he had married, but Muthu had stood with her mom in all the difficult times.

Even when Vasundhara's relatives blamed her for the break up, whenever she had to meet them on some occasion or other, which sent her back home wounded and hurt, Muthu was there to console and tell her that it was her life and that she had the right to judge not others. She never let her break down. It's not an exaggeration, to say that she also played an important role along with her mother in bringing the family to a respectable position. Muthu always believed that a day would come for Vasundhara to prove the people of her mettle and amaze them with her accomplishments.

Vasundhara's friends felt that Muthu's loyalty was due to the help she got from Vasundhara. But Vasundhara, Megha and Bharathi knew that Muthu's loyalty wasn't love for money. It was unselfish love. She never expected anything from them. Weighing that love in terms of money would belittle that beautiful bond. Even in this materialistic world, we sometimes do come across some souls who live for love. Muthu saw Megha immersed deep in thoughts. So she did not ask anything but went inside the kitchen and started sorting out the things. She called out from the kitchen, "Megha, do you want coffee or tea? What did you eat in the hospital? Did you take anything? Are you hungry?" Megha did not answer. She sat staring at the walls again ruminating over the thoughts, since the time her father entered.

Muthu did not wait for an answer too. Those were asked for the sake of asking. She came with two cups of tea. She handed over a cup and sat opposite to her drinking from her cup of tea. She asked, "What did the doctor say? What happened to Amma? How is she? Did you see her in the morning?" She would have continued, if Megha had continued her silence.

Megha told her, sobbing in between, what the doctor had told. Muthu consoled her saying that everything would get well soon, as God never punished good people, though he might test them with some hurdles. She asked her, "Why did your father come that day? What did he say?". Muthu knew her father as she had been working in their house, since Megha's birth. Muthu always felt that Vasundhara was too soft towards him. When he left, Vasundhara shifted to a smaller house with her girls.

Muthu continued to work in their house, though it was far from the place she resided. She did not want to leave Vasundhara alone at the time of distress. Vasundhara asked Muthu to find work elsewhere, as she won't be able to pay her with her salary. Muthu told her lovingly that Vasundhara had mistaken her. She did not work for money, but, for the love she got from Vasundhara.

Muthu told Vasundhara that she wasn't ready to leave her alone, when Vasundhara's life was in doldrums. She also told Vasundhara that she can pay her whenever she could and whatever she could afford. She took care of Megha and Bharathi, when they got back from school until Vasundhara returned from college without being asked to do so.

Slowly Vasundhara came out of the frustrations and pains caused by her husband and other people around. She paid for Nirmala's education which according to Muthu was a waste. When Nirmala started showing very good results in school, she stopped talking against Nirmala's education. Muthu refused the salary Vasundhara paid her, so Vasundhara started an account in Muthu's name in a bank and deposited the money for her future use.

Muthu worked in three more houses in addition to Vasundhara's place. Her husband was a drunkard who beat her and wasted the money she had saved for the kids' food on drinks. Once when they were all away, he sold Nirmala's books and a few vessels they had at home. The enraged Muthu threw him out of her life, as she thought that he was incorrigible. With two kids after Nirmala, she decided that she could do better without him. Nirmala was in the tenth standard then, and ready to write her public exams.

Whether they are educated or uneducated, Megha sometimes felt, men were cheaters and selfish. For them it was only their happiness and ego that was more important than the wife who had come trusting them or the kids who depended solely on them. But Vasundhara did not encourage those ideas in Megha. She said that attitudes differed from person to person, be it a male or a female and generalisation is not true.A few examples cannot be used as the yard stick to judge the whole society.

Two years back, once when Muthu was crossing the road, a speeding bike hit her. After this accident, she was unable to walk for almost a year. Now she can walk, but still had pain and a limp. The doctors had advised her from doing any hard work. Seeing Megha again immersed in her own thoughts, Muthu did not want to discuss anything further. She asked Megha whether she had taken her breakfast. She did not wait for her answer but went inside the kitchen to prepare something.

Muthu opened the refrigerator to see, if dosa batter was there. She knew that Vasundhara always kept some stock of it, as it came handy and was easy to prepare. Seeing a small bowl of batter left, she took it out and allowed it to come to room temperature. Meanwhile, she cut onion and chillies which she added to the dough along with some wheat flour. While whipping it, she remembered the gloomy day five years back. It was as silent as this day, but Vasundhara was there along with Megha. Bharathi had just been employed.

The same uncomfortable silence encircled their family and she was standing in the kitchen preparing food, unable to bear the pain of both the women who sat in misery with the unfortunate turn of things that took place that day. Megha's younger sister Bharathi was angry. Megha was 25 years old, when that incident happened.

Ramgopal worked in the physics department in the college where Megha worked. He was attracted towards Megha from the day he set his eyes on her. He proposed to her. As Megha did not have any intentions to get married, she did not want to entertain him.

Both the girls did not have any idea of getting married. But, Vasundhara vetoed their opinion. She tried driving in the point that all men need not be bad just because their father was bad. She tried hard to change the attitude of her girls. She once expressed her fear about her daughters to Muthu. Muthu waved it away saying that things would change, when they would meet their Mr. Perfect. Vasundhara too hoped for that day to come. The day did come but did not turn out to be a happy moment at all.

Shaking away her thoughts, Muthu came out with the dosas and chutney and served Megha. Megha refused, "I will first bathe. I am feeling tired and exhausted. I am not hungry." Muthu forced her to eat. Megha said, "OK, then you also eat with me." Megha struggled with one dosa which refused to pass down her throat. Muthu sat with the dosa in her plate untouched, watching Megha with sorrow. She asked God in her heart as to why he had to give so many troubles to such a nice and kind family.

She remembered Vasundhara's explanation to this, whenever she lamented about some problem. Gold is beaten, put in fire and goes through all troubles before becoming a jewel in the showcase of a shop or on the crown of Lord. Life is always a journey of troubles and failures to make us mature and shining.

Megha told Muthu, "Ma, I am going to pack and take food for lunch for Nirmala and myself. After I finish my work in college, I will go to the hospital to see how amma is doing. Then after lunch, I need to go to the hospital to see Bharathi. The doctor has called me to see her."

Muthu said, "I will prepare lunch for you both. I will bring it to the hospital around one in the afternoon." Muthu was silent for a few minutes then she asked, "Megha, can I come with you to see Bharathi?" Muthu felt that it would be a moral support for Megha, if she was around. Moreover she did not want to send Megha alone. Megha felt a wave of relief sweep her. She readily accepted the idea, though she knew that it would be a strain on Muthu.

Megha went to bathe. She remembered how Muthu had always been there, whenever she confronted problems. When she was just 10 years old, one day she came home weeping from school when a friend of hers teased her. Muthu told her to face the friend instead of crying. Muthu taught her that running away will only make them tease her more. She came with her to school the next day to ensure that she wasn't teased anymore.

She remembered the day, she came home all confused and scared, when she attained puberty. With her mom in college, it was Muthu who pacified her and made her understand. Muthu was so happy. Usually she left their house by five in the evening, but that day she stayed until six and waited for Vasundhara to return from college. She came the next day with lot of flowers and glass bangles which Megha loved.

She was there when Megha's marriage became a flop show. She was there when Bharathi decided to end her life and her mom was in tears not knowing what had happened to her. Now again, she was there when Megha thought that she was all alone. She went into the kitchen to help Muthu. But, Muthu was half way through with cooking.

Megha remembered that she was always agile, perfect and maintained cleanliness. Everyone in their house loved the way she worked. Above all, she was a very honest person. She never took a pie more than what was due to her. Megha had seen people with money being dishonest. Her mom always said that honesty had nothing to do with poverty or richness

Megha asked Muthu to take an auto to come to the hospital. Muthu refused saying that she would take the bus. Megha forced her and gave her the money and left for her college. The journey towards unknown future started for Megha. The lines of Theodere Tilson entered her mind without her permission.

"Pain is hard to bear;" he cried"
But with patience, day by day,
EVEN THIS WILL PASS AWAY."

TIDE 10

Megha stood in the bus stand watching people being busy with their chores. She boarded the bus that surprisingly came on time. Eleven in the morning usually saw the buses less crowded unless and until there were festivities in the temples that were on the way to her college. She never had the luxury of choosing a seat, as she usually travelled in the peak hours. She took a seat near the window. She watched the roads, the markets and the shops, all crowded. The bus stopped in front of a marriage hall located near a bus stop to take in people and spit some out. A few ladies dressed in costly silks and jewels that adorned their necks and ears boarded the bus with children, all dressed in silk skirts and flowers that adorned their hair. Happiness was smeared on their faces with smiles sprinkled all over their face. They were all talking at the same time. They sat down in the vacant seats. Megha saw that all the seats were now filled up. The whole bus smelled of perfumes and jasmines. She was reminded of the day, she was to get married five years ago, when she was a bride, dressed in a similar way. That day, which she had expected eagerly and enthusiastically, ended with sorrow and tears. That special day saw her both in extreme happiness and in tremendous sorrow.

Megha never wanted to get married. She had seen her mom suffer in her father's hands. She had come to know from her married friends about the indifference of the husbands after the marriage. Of course there were some who led a happy and successful married life and who supported their wives to achieve their dreams. But that number was very less compared to the people who failed to understand their partners. From her mom, she came to know that her father too was very appreciative about her lectures and work before the marriage, but the same man wanted her to quit giving lectures, though he knew that her mom put her life and soul in her work.

Ramgopal, was the name of the man whom she was to wed. As she never had the idea of getting married, she did not encourage people talking about her marriage or about a prospective groom. Ramgopal once asked her the way to the physics department and introduced himself as the newly recruited lecturer of the physics department in Megha's college. She saw some students walking towards the department, so she asked them to take him to the physic department. He uttered a thank you, while walking away with the students. She forgot this incident after that moment.

But Ramgopal remembered and the next day wished her at first, when she entered the college. He started having small conversations with her. Megha at first thought that it was just a coincidence. But later she found out that he was creating opportunities to interact with her. Her friend, Sumithra, a lecturer in her department told her that she felt that the guy was trying to become friendly with her. She tried avoiding him, but he was a hard nut. One day he came to her and said that he wanted to talk to her. She replied that she had nothing to talk to him.

He found an opportunity, when she was alone and proposed to her. Megha got very wild. She told him, "I don't believe in love at first sight. What do you know about me, Mr.Ramgopal that you are proposing to me?. I don't know anything about you either and what made you think that I will accept your proposal?. Being a mentor to my students, I personally think that you have selected a very wrong place, a college to propose. Please do not entertain such ideas in your mind. I am not interested." and walked away.

Ramgopal who did not expect this response was shocked. He did not talk to Megha after that. She was happy that she had driven sense in Ramgopal's mind. She forgot this matter completely. One Sunday, when she returned home from her friend's place, she found a car outside the house and a few pairs of slippers. She wondered who could be the visitors and rang the bell. Bharathi opened the door. Megha saw a couple talking to her mother and was shocked to find Ramgopal seated in a chair near her mom.

She walked past them into the other room with Bharathi following her. Bharathi told her, "Megha, they have come to ask for your hand in marriage for their son. He is a physics lecturer in your college. Do you know him Megha?" Megha told Bharathi about his proposing to her and her refusing it. Bharathi laughed saying, "he has found another way to marry you, darling. His mom was telling amma that he was madly in love with you and they would take care of you very well. They said that they would help you pursue your dreams and would not hinder your career plans."

Megha asked Bharathi, "Why do they want to discuss so many things, when I don't want to marry that guy?" Her mom said to them that she would discuss with Megha and let them know her wish. She heard Ramgopal saying, "Take your time, aunty, but give me a positive reply. I promise to give her only happiness." The mother of Ramgopal was telling Vasundhara, "My son was so impressed with your daughter that he wants to marry her. He has decided that he will marry none other than your daughter. So give me a good reply."

Megha waited for them to leave. She told her mom that she had already refused him, when he proposed and that it was highly indecent of him to compel her into marrying him.Her mom did not say anything at that time. But talked to her after a few hours, when Megha had cooled down and was ready to hear her mother talk. She said, "Megha, the family is good. He too seems to be good. Tell me why you don't like him?". She fell silent for she did not have reason to hate him, but she did not want to marry either. Her mom told her, "I think he is a nice person Megha, as he has come with his parents to ask for you." "But I told him amma that I don't want to marry him. Why did he come?"

After a few days, Ramgopal and his parents started contacting her mom. His parents became closer to her mom. He started coming to her house to talk to her mom. Slowly, Megha too accepted him. She finally agreed for the marriage. Vasundhara wanted the marriage to be conducted only in the registrar's office. Then she wanted to take the newlyweds to a temple for blessings of God. She wasn't for a grand marriage. But Ramgopal's mom told," I have only one child. I want the marriage to be conducted in a grand way. We can conduct the marriage in a temple according to the customs of our community. We will hold a grand reception. I want my son's marriage to be conducted in a grand style."

Vasundhara agreed. She booked a mantap in an old temple of Lord Muruga in the city. The groom's parents' wanted three rooms to be booked in a hotel near the temple for their relatives. That too was done. Then Megha told Ram about her principle not to wear silk. He said, "Oh Megha, that is so nice. I agree with you. But, my mom, she loves silk. So wear it for the wedding. Later you can stick to your principles. I will support you." Megha compromised.

Ramgopal said that he was in love with Megha, but did everything the way he and his parents wanted. Megha did not suspect his love, neither did Vasundhara. But Bharathi did get wild, whenever the grooms' side made demands. The marriage day, the seventh of April arrived in all splendours and the house wore a festive look. Vasundhara, Muthu and her sons went first to arrange the things in the mantap, while Nirmala and Bharathi went along with Megha just two hours before the ceremony that was to take place in the evening before the wedding day.

Megha wore a copper sulphate coloured Mysore silk sari with dark ink blue border which she bought for the occasion. She wore ear studs and a simple string made of turquoise that matched her sari. She wore blue glass bangles. She braided her long hair and clipped strings of jasmine flowing on it. She remembered the way her friends and mom admired her beauty. Her hands were adorned with Mehendi. It was made by grinding henna leaves freshly plucked. She wore it three days before her wedding. When she removed the henna, the palms looked deep red. Muthu smilingly told that the mehendi goes red only on the hands of the maiden whose husband is loving. The myth did not prove right in her life. Ramgopal was handsome and looked a perfect match for her. He was all smiles for his dreams were turning true.

The day of marriage dawned with everything golden and sweet in Megha's eyes. The auspicious moment for tying the knot was from nine to ten in the morning. Vasundhara was bubbling with joy. Muthu was happy to see the family finally very happy. When Megha walked out from the dressing room in a deep maroon saree embroidered with golden flowers, she could see everyone gaping at her. She remembered her mom kissing her saying that she looked beautiful. The whole marriage hall smelt of jasmine and perfume just as it smells in the bus now. She walked slowly accompanied by Bharathi and Nirmala and sat near her husband to be, Ram. She was so happy and excited. The pundits started chanting the mantras. Suddenly Ram began to sweat professedly and swooned. She couldn't understand anything that took place after that as there was big commotion and chaos. Nirmala, being a doctor came running to the spot with a cup of water. Ram did not regain consciousness. Nirmala saw that his pulse was also very weak. So she took Ram to the hospital immediately. With Bharathi, Vasundhara and Nirmala away, Megha was left alone with Muthu and the people who came to attend the marriage. She could hear people blame her luck. She did not know how to react. She felt as if she was brutally woken up from a very good dream.

The trio returned from hospital, but maintained stoic silence. Vasundhara told the people who had come for the wedding that the wedding was called off, as Ramgopal was sick. When Muthu asked Vasundhara the reason, she hushed her away saying that they could talk everything at home. Megha walked like a doll towards the car and stayed silent wondering what the problem was.

Bharathi said," They cheated us, Megha. It seems Ram is having some problem in his heart right from his birth. He has been taking treatment for it. The doctors had advised him against getting married. Ramgopal and his parents have knowingly played with your life, Megha. We need to complain to police." Megha felt cheated. If only had

Ramgopal told her the truth, there was a chance of her accepting him. But now, she felt so bad. Vasundhara made a wrong decision once again believing their words getting deceived by the way they talked. That was the time, when Vasundhara shed tears of sorrow seeing Megha.

Megha couldn't believe her ears. She wanted to ask many questions, like "why did he want to marry then? Why did he not tell me about his health? Why were his parents silent too?". She couldn't ask and she didn't. She was depressed. She wanted to quit the college, as she did not want to see him. Megha blamed her fate.

Vasundhara, hugged her tenderly and said, "Whatever has happened, has happened for good darling. It is a good thing that we did not come to know of his health after the marriage. Come on Megha, why should you quit the college. It is the person who hid the truth must quit."

When Ram's father came the next day to apologise, for that was what he said, Vasundhara told him that she prayed for Ram's good health and she did not want to discuss any further. Then he asked Vasundhara to send her daughter Megha with him, as Ram wanted to talk to her.

Vasundhara called Megha. Even now Megha felt surprised by the reply she gave. She told him, "I cannot come to see your son. Had he told me the truth, maybe I would have married him. But he is dishonest. What is there to talk to me? I am really sorry for hurting you with my words. I pray for his good health."

When Ram's father asked her to reconsider her decision not to meet Ram, she retorted "Will you consider, if I were your daughter facing a similar situation?" She went inside her room thus closing the conversation. Ramgopal tried talking to her in the college, but she stood stern. When he came to visit Vasundhara, she asked him not to trouble them anymore and put an end to the whole relationship that had not even started to bloom.

This incident made her mom breakdown and cry. She felt so hurt to see her daughter being called unlucky. It took quite a long time for Megha to forget him and the event. "It is funny" Megha mused, "the society always accused the girl, be it divorce or rape or eve teasing. Eventually it is the girls who is made to bear the brunt. The society points its fingers towards the victims calling them unlucky, arrogant, and not properly dressed or tempted the person. No one is ready to punish the person who wronged, but ready to heap insults on the afflicted girl". She was reminded of the lines her mom told when she cursed her fate, which stands apt in this situation too . . . .

> *Be still, sad heart, and cease repining;*
> *Behind the clouds is the sun still shining;*
> *Thy fate is the common fate of all,*
> *Into each life some rain must fall,*
> *Some days must be dark and dreary*

She was nudged by the lady near her who got up to alight. A small girl who was standing till then sat down. When she turned to see her, the girl smiled at her and showed her bangles proudly. She smiled at the girl enjoying her innocence. Megha thought, "How nice it will be to remain at that age of the girl forever!" The bus was nearing her college. She waved to the kid and got ready to alight. Her college wasn't very far from the bus stop. She walked on the narrow platform and reached the entrance of her college. Her Saraswathi college of arts and science had a lot of greenery around. It housed many rare species of trees and birds. There were deers and monkeys. Sometimes she had had the luck of spying a peacock dance. Megha reached the office, intimated them about her leave. She walked down the corridor up the stairs to her department. She told the head of the department about her mother. Her colleagues wanted to visit her mom. She told them that it wasn't possible as her mom was in the ICU. So one of the friends who commuted to college by car said that she would take her to the hospital. She gave the corrected answer papers to one of her colleagues for distributing to the students. When they drove towards the hospital, her heart had big hopes in it as she believed in her mom's words, that the sun will shine when the clouds pass.

When she reached the hospital, it was nearing one in the afternoon. She walked to the ICU and waited for Nirmala to come out. Nirmala told Megha that her mom was sleeping. Muthu had come to the hospital before her on time with the packed lunch. Muthu decided to sit outside the ICU, while Nirmala and Megha wanted to go for lunch. But Muthu said that she wasn't hungry.

Nirmala and Megha both went to the canteen to have their lunch. It wasn't crowded. They settled down in a bench which was facing the garden. The canteen wasn't actually a building. It just had a acrylic sheet cover for the ceiling with a few pillars to support it. There was a Nescafe machine and light snacks were available. Nirmala went to get water, while Megha opened one of the boxes, Muthu had packed. There were rotis and potato curry. Another box had curd rice with some pickle.

She gazed at the garden. There were two wood peckers pecking hard on the trunk of a banyan tree which spread its wide branches showing off its terrestrial roots hanging all over it. Every peck emitted a metallic sound which was answered by a peck by the another woodpecker. Its red crown opened and closed like a fan with every movement. There was a small pond near the tree which was abundant with lotus blooms and a few lilies that were blue making the pond colourful. The gardener was clearing the weeds and watering the plants. One woodpecker stopped as if it was tired and needed a break. The other one went on with its job. The one which decided to rest flew and went near the busy one. It kept gazing at first, and then slowly pecked its neck. The busy one shrugged its wings and went on with its work. The idle one now flew over and dropped sharp at the busy one pecking it on its crown. The annoyed busy bird opened its crown to its full and uttered some screams and gave the teaser a peck on its body. It flew away. She felt curious to see what had gone between them. Nirmala's voice brought her back to earth from the paradise which soothes the worries. They both had rotis and curd rice.

Nirmala told Megha, "Amma will be discharged in two days. My mom can attend to Vasundhara Amma when you go to college. I will come and relieve my mom when I am on night shifts, Megha." Megha did not have any words to speak. A small word "thanks" will surely hurt her. When she had thanked Muthu once, when Muthu helped her, she asked Megha immediately whether she would thank her mom for everything she did. She asked emotionally why she had to thank her, if she thought her as a part of her family. Megha never used the word, when she came to know that it was distancing them from her. Even without her asking and even before she thought of managing things, Nirmala had planned ahead. What did her family do to them? She studied, Muthu worked and they succeeded all because of their own efforts. Nirmala called out, "Eh! Megha! Don't brood. Everything will become normal soon. I have the confidence."

Nirmala was happy that her mother was accompanying Megha to meet Bharathi. She told Megha "Do not become emotional in front of Bharathi. Be calm." They both were worried about what to say, if Bharathi asked about her mom. Megha remembered the book her mom was working on. She was planning to publish the poems she had written and Bharathi too knew it. So it was decided that Bharathi would be told that Vasundhara had gone to meet the publishers in Mumbai who had agreed to bring out her work. The time was 2 PM, when they finished their lunch. Muthu had coffee and biscuits. Megha and Muthu left as it would take almost an hour to reach the hospital where Bharathi was admitted. She did not want be late for the appointment.

TIDE 11

Megha and Muthu called an auto, as there wasn't any straight bus for the hospital that was located a bit away from the city. Megha was afraid that they might be late. They reached the hospital which had tall iron gates with security personnel sitting near them to prevent the in patients from running away. Megha thought of the life inside the solid gates. It's terrible. We seldom realise our blessings and lament about trivial issues. They both walked into the reception and enquired about their appointment giving Bharathi's name.

They were asked to wait in the visitors' room till the doctor came. There were three other visitors waiting in the room to meet Dr. Shivashankar. Everyone had his/her own share of problems and pains. The lady who sat opposite to her smiled at her. When Megha smiled back, the lady asked Megha, if she was visiting a patient. As if the lady wanted to pour out her woes to someone, she did not wait for Megha's answer, but went on telling her story without pausing.

"My son is treated here for pszysophrenia. He was a very brilliant boy. There was nothing abnormal in him. He was smart and intelligent. He finished his masters in science with a gold medal and came home two years back. He wanted to pursue his research abroad. So he was applying to various universities. My son had many friends, but slowly he started avoiding them. He became a psychopath. We did not see anything unusual, as we thought he was busy with his application process. He became a poor eater and sometimes went without food. He never slept. When he started neglecting his personal hygiene, we started to get concerned".

"One day last August, he jumped from the balcony of our house. It was in the second floor. He escaped with a few fractures and he was treated for it. He started behaving in a weird way. He said that people were scheming against him. They were plotting to kill him. He hallucinated."

"We took him to many hospitals where several tablets that suppressed his hallucination were given. It made him sleep for a long time. But he did not get better. The doctors gave him electric shock treatment. But it had given only short term results". We took him for counselling but it was made in a routine and my son reiterated whatever he thought was right. My husband who had the patience till then started accusing him being lazy. This made the matters worse. I came to know about Ashraye from a friend of mine. I asked my husband to take our son there, but he washed his hands off him. I can understand that the treatment costs a lot and it needed a lot of patience and first of all acceptance. But where will he go, if we deny him support. So I brought my son here. The doctor told me that my son has started talking normally. I am so happy. Sometimes God is very cruel Ma,. Where will my son go if his family disowns him?." She wiped her tears that were flowing down her cheeks.

A person born disabled is accepted by all, but people who get afflicted by mental illness in the midway are not accepted and it's pathetic. India, that way Megha thought, wasn't friendly to the people with these special problems. There aren't steps in buses that are comfortable for disabled people or senior citizens to board or alight. The railway stations have steep staircases and climbing them is one big ordeal. None including the government bothers about these people. In the case of mentally disabled, people don't seem to understand or appreciate the problems faced by the individual or their family. They look down on them as if they are sinners.

The afflicted people are blamed and teased for no mistake of theirs. Even the parents consider such kids as a burden. Very few special kids are lucky to have parents who are supportive. Others do not appreciate the pain of the children or adults having these disorders and shun them. She had heard from Dr.Shivashankar that many patients are forced to stay in the hospital even after their recovery, as the parents are reluctant to take them back

The nurse came in to call the lady who had been talking to Megha. Another half an hour passed and Megha was called in. She left Muthu behind and went to meet the doctor. The doctor enquired about her mother. Dr. Shivashankar told, "Please be seated. You need to remember certain things, when you converse with your sister. First of all, I will advise you not to talk about her past. Don't tell Bharathi about your mom's condition. She has recovered a lot, but I don't want to take chances. Allow her to talk. Let us see how she reacts on seeing you. Megha! What are you going to say if she asks about your mom?" Megha replied, "I am going to tell her that mom has gone to Mumbai to meet a publisher who has decided to publish her works. Doctor, she will believe it as she knows that mom was working on a book." Then she said "Our friend Muthu has also come to see Bharathi. Can I take her too doctor?" The doctor asked Megha to go and meet Bharathi first and then she could take Muthu also to see Bharathi.

Megha was taken inside the ward by a man who wore a white uniform. Bharathi gave a surprised look. She came running and hugged her. She asked Megha "Where is amma?" Megha replied calmly, trying not to show any emotion," Amma has gone to Mumbai, Bharathi . . . to see a publisher about publishing her book. Remember, she has completed it". Megha expected to see disappointment in Bharathi's eyes. But Bharathi was so happy that their mom had finally completed her work and was going to publish her poems.

She told Megha, "I want to hear mom recite the poems Megha". It was a big surprise to Megha. Bharathi smiled on seeing surprise creep into Megha's eyes. She asked Megha, "Why do you look so dull and tired. Are you ill?". Megha gulped the words and said it was due to heat outside. Bharathi told her about the other patients in the ward. She talked about the doctor, the nurses and the attenders. It was so nice to hear her talk after a long time.

She showed a notebook. She said she was helping the doctor on a project. "Dr. Shivashankar wanted to create awareness among the public about mental sickness. He wanted to visit villages and treat children and adults who are afflicted with mental illness. As this hospital is too small to accommodate many people who need attention, the doctor and his friend are planning to build another hospital."

She asked about Nirmala. Bharathi said she wanted to meet her and get her help too. Megha felt as if she was in some dream world, when Bharathi told her that she would go for a job in three months. She would be helping Dr. Shivashankar with 75% of her salary. She had never heard Bharathi speak that way. It was surprise after surprise, when she saw the book of Bhagavat Gita lying on her table. Megha touched the book. Bharathi told her that she was reading the book and it was marvellous.

She told Megha "I did not realise the true value of Gita until I read it." Dr. Shivashankar sent Muthu in. Megha told her that Muthu had come. Bharathi was happy. They both exchanged emotional glances for a moment. She asked Muthu to bring samosas, when she would come next time. That is when Megha realised that she hadn't brought anything for Bharathi in her frenzy. Muthu handed over a box to her. Megha was surprised. The box contained rotis and potato curry. Bharathi was very delighted. She started eating like a small kid. Muthu said, "Bharathi I will bring you samosas tomorrow".

Bharathi replied smiling, "I need 50 ma, I have to give all my friends here".That really was a tremendous recovery Bharathi had made, Megha mused. She missed her mom a lot. Bharathi on seeing that it was getting late asked Megha to leave. She asked Muthu to take care of her darling sister who seemed sick and was hiding something from her. Megha reiterated with a pleasant smile that she wasn't dull at all. Waving a goodbye to her sister and promising to meet her with samosas, she was about to leave, when Bharathi called her again. She asked Megha to bring her laptop also during her next visit.

Megha agreed to bring the laptop and parted with a small peck on her cheeks and a soft kiss. Megha's heart was happy about Bharathi's recovery but was sad to think of her mom. How was she going to break this news to Bharathi? How will she take it? Will she again slip into the shell? Shivashankar was happy with Bharathi. He too told Megha about Bharathi's help in his project and many other things that involved his patients. He told her another surprising thing that Bharathi actually spent most of her time with patients giving inspirational talks.

Sometimes the people you least expect perform deeds you ever dream of. She really felt proud of Bharathi. Dr. Shivashankar asked them to meet Bharathi on next Sunday. Muthu and Megha walked out to the selfish world through the iron gates. Megha turned back to see the building which housed people who did not have time to think of themselves, who suffered in silence and who weren't accepted as human beings at all by the people where she came from.

She saw the lady, who had been talking to her in the visiting room, coming out of the hospital. She waved at Muthu and Megha to stop. She was so happy to say that her son had talked to her. The doctor had told her that with counselling and treatment her son would be able to get back to work. Megha took the lady and Muthu to a hotel nearby and discussed about their problems, while they drank coffee.

TIDE 12

Megha and Muthu boarded a bus to the terminus. From the terminus, Megha had to catch a bus to go to the hospital and Muthu had to take another bus going in a different direction. Muthu's bus came first. Megha's bus came after a few minutes and it was less crowded. She boarded the bus and took the seat behind a mom with a small kid. When the bus started moving, wind slapped on her face. The small girl stood on the seat and started waving at Megha. Megha too waved.

The girl smiled at first and then bent down. She thought that the kid was playing hide and seek. But she came up with a handkerchief with Donald Duck printed on it. She showed it proudly. Then again she bent down to retrieve something. When she got up, she showed two bars of chocolates and laughed. Her mom saw what was going on. She told Megha proudly that her kid was showing her the things she had brought. Megha smiled and patted the kid on her cheeks. She asked her name. The kid in her beautiful baby tone said "Vaishali". Vaishali now was preoccupied with her handkerchief and a small doll her mom had got her.

That is the beauty of innocence. Unlike a child, we are never content with what we have. Greed, anger and avarice, conquer and corrupt our mind and hearts as we grow up that we find it difficult to converse with anyone with such ease. We are unable to enjoy the simple things in life. We always yearn for the things we are unable to get or don't deserve.

One smile from a kid can turn any moment into eternal bliss. It was past visitors' time, when Megha reached the hospital. Disappointed, Megha sat in one of chairs that were outside the ICU. She saw Nirmala coming from the other end. She asked Megha, "Eh! When did you get back? How is Bharathi? Did she talk?"

Before answering the questions posed by Nirmala, Megha asked, "Can I see amma?". "No", Nirmala responded. "It's past visitors' time. They won't allow you unless there is any emergency.". Nirmala told her, "Megha! Amma woke up, but there wasn't any change. She did not speak or ask the question she was asking us. She was trying to get up. So I made her sit.

I asked her, if she wanted to drink something. She did not reply. So I gave her a cup of water. She could not hold the cup, Megha, but when I placed it on her lips, she drank it. So I went to ask the doctor, if we can give her something to drink like juice or porridge." The doctor said that we can try giving her, when he comes to see amma around eight during his night rounds. Megha, we can try to get permission to get you in. Don't worry". It was only seven in the night. They still had an hour before the doctor's visit. So Nirmala planned to finish her dinner with Megha. They both walked towards the canteen.

Nirmala smiled at Megha, "Will you now tell me about Bharathi darling?" Megha became very happy and enthusiastic, when she started talking about Bharathi. She told her everything. Megha continued, "Bharathi talked very cheerfully and with confidence. Bharathi asked for samosas too to share with her friends." Nirmala too told happily that it clearly showed that she was getting back to normal. She also told Nirmala about the lady, the mother of a paranoid son, she met in the hospital.

Nirmala told that she had seen many cases like this. She too agreed that we never give respect or help people or the relatives of these special people. That needs a lot of awareness she said. Nirmala said," Dr. Shivashankar is doing a good service to these people. He had started this institution with his friend Mr. Suryakumar, who helps him a lot in managing things. He is an MBA. He had a neighbour who had a kid afflicted with bipolar disease".

Megha asked her "A what". Nirmala enlightened Megha, "We all have our ups and downs, but, with bipolar disorder, these peaks and valleys are more severe. The symptoms of bipolar disorder can hurt your job and school performance, damage your relationships, and disrupt your daily life. And although it's treatable, many people don't recognize the warning signs and get the help they need. Since bipolar disorder tends to worsen without treatment, we are unable to save many of them".

Megha shivered, "It is really terrible to hear. I have never known such diseases exist. Life must be very difficult for these people."

Nirmala continued, "Unable to understand the boy's sickness, the parents at first thought he was being lazy. Then they came to think it was some curse. They took him to all the temples and did a lot of poojas. The boy was an adult and his illness got worse. The parents felt insulted at the way the boy behaved. They had a daughter who was very good in studies and health. They did not have the patience to take care of their son. They left him in a temple which sheltered a lot of people like him. In that place the sick were chained and beaten to drive away the evil spirits. The boy suffered a lot in their hands and finally died."

Nirmala paused, "In a way, Megha, death gave him freedom from this harassment and a torturous life. Seeing this Suryakumar who was an undergraduate then, decided to come up in life and do something for these special people". He had this doctor friend, Shivashankar, who too had the same ideals as his".

"This is the story behind the organisation "Ashraya". It was started in a small house which had just two rooms. Slowly it grew in size. Actually every week Suryakumar travelled with some of the volunteers to nearby villages and towns to identify these people. He had saved many who were awfully wounded and unconscious. Some were from very good families who did not want to have a black mark with them. Suryakumar is a MBA running a consultancy of his own. He uses half of his salary for this project." Nirmala took a deep breath before telling Megha, "the world is still green and prosperous because of people like Vasundhara, Suryakumar, Shivashankar and their likes."

Megha remembered Bharathi telling her about a project in which she wanted to help the doctor. Nirmala smiled saying that Bharathi will be back to her heels. Megha spelt out her fear about facing Bharathi next time, when she would ask about her mom. But Nirmala rubbed it off saying that everything will happen well, when the time comes and the doctor knew that she is strong enough to take in these things. They finished dining. They both walked towards the ICU, when a nurse who was coming out of the ICU told them that she had kept the juice ready for Vasundhara. They both sat chatting about Bharathi and waited for the doctor to arrive.

Around ten minutes past eight Dr. Subramanian came. He smiled and asked Megha about her sister. She replied that she was getting better. Megha did not know, if she would I be allowed in the ICU; but she very much wanted to see her mom. Nirmala and the doctor entered the ICU. Doctor turned back and asked Megha to come in. Megha thanked him.

Vasundhara was wide awake. She was meddling with the bed sheet. When Megha called her, she did not look towards her. Doctor patted on her hands. She looked up at him. He asked her what her name was. She stared to reply first then fell into pensive silence as if she was thinking about something. Nirmala asked her, "Amma, do you want to drink something? Are you hungry?" Vasundhara kept on seeing Nirmala's lip movements, but did not answer. Megha called her "Amma, drink some juice". She gave the same look.

Nirmala poured a portion of the orange juice in a tumbler and gave her. She saw it with curiosity. It looked as though she was seeing the tumbler for the first time. Megha helped her grip the tumbler. She pulled her hands away. Now Nirmala brought the tumbler to her lips. When the juice touched her lips, she drank it. She kept gazing at the tumbler, so Nirmala poured some more juice and gave her. This time she opened her mouth, when the tumbler went near her mouth.

The doctor told Megha that they could try solid food the next day and then shift her to the general ward. In a way, her mom was better than the day before. Megha thought that she might get better in a few weeks time. Doctor Subramanian went to check on other patients. Megha and Nirmala came out as Vasundhara looking at them with curiosity, as if she was seeing some strange people from an alien planet. One thing they both noticed about mom was that she had stopped talking.

Megha asked Nirmala to go home. Nirmala had been in hospital all day long. Megha thought that it wasn't fair to ask her to stay, though she would have felt happy to have Nirmala around. She waved her goodnight and sat in a chair outside the ICU. There wasn't anyone other than her. She closed her eyes and recounted that day which had been an oasis in the desert. She thought about the services rendered by Suryakumar. She did not know when she fell asleep.

She was woken up by the bustle of nurses and the people around busily sweeping and mopping the place. It was five in the morning. The posture had made her legs and neck stiff. She went to wash her face and freshen herself. When she returned, she saw a nurse coming out of the room. She asked about her mom. The nurse told her that her mom had been awake for a long time in the night, but now she was asleep. When Megha asked her when she would be able to meet her mom, she replied that the doctor would come to check on her around nine in the morning and she would be permitted in at that time. Having nothing to do, but wait, she walked down the steps to the canteen. She had a hot cup of tea.

The hospital had a huge garden with a variety of flowers. There were birds that were screeching at the top of their voices wishing the patients good luck. When she was about to go back, she saw the lady with the kid whom she had met in the visitors' room the day before. Megha enquired about her husband. She replied that he was getting better and was responding well to the medicines. She introduced herself as Shakti.

Shakti enquired about Megha's mom. When Megha replied that she was a bit better than the day before, Shakti told her not to lose hope and faith. "No one can predict what is in store for us the next moment. For all you know, your mom will be back on her foot by the end of the day. The doctors thought that my husband will not survive. But his will power and his love towards our kid and me, made him fight and get back. Now he is stable", she paused. She told this boldly and happily, but her eyes had tears that expressed the struggles within her.

"How scared she would have been when doctors had given up hope?" Megha thought. She should be thankful to God, if the doctors did not say anything negative about her mom. She felt a surge of hope rush into her. She thanked Shakti, wished her all luck and walked towards the ICU to see her mom. She sat waiting for the doctor to arrive. She prayed that her mom should be sent to the general ward so that she can be by her side. The other beneficial thing in moving to the general ward was that it would bring some hope that her mom was getting better.

ICU looked very scary. She lost her confidence and courage, when she walked into it. She wanted her mom out of that creepy room as soon as possible. She thought of the people who had more sufferings and pains in life. She was lucky to have problems that could be sorted out easily.

If everything went well and her mom was brought to general ward, she thought that she would take the laptop to Bharathi on Sunday. She reminded herself to get some sweets which Bharathi loved. She still was surprised at the way Bharathi talked. It was different. "What would have changed her? "she wondered. She doubted, if they would ever come to know what had troubled her in USA. She brushed away those thoughts saying that it wasn't important. What was important was to get Bharathi back to normalcy.

A booming voice saying, "Good morning" shook her out of her thoughts and made her land on earth. Dr. Subramanian stood before her. She too wished him with a smile. They both entered the ICU. Megha woke her mom up. She got up immediately. The doctor talked to her with zero response from the other side. There was a small change in her. Vasundhara did not have the fear in her eyes. She kept watching with amusement the people moving around.

They offered her water. She drank it, but couldn't hold the tumbler, as on earlier day. The doctor wanted to try solid food. The nurse brought a plate of idli. When Megha took a piece and kept it on her lips, she opened her mouth and ate it slowly chewing on it. She had three pieces and then refused to open her mouth further.

The Doctor asked Megha to give her something to eat in small intervals. He also decided to shift her to the general ward, as she did not have any problem swallowing food or drinking liquids. Vasundhara was gaping at both of them, while they were conversing. Did she understand or was she just looking at them was what Megha was curious to know. Dr. Subramanian filled up her mom's chart. He asked Megha, if she was going home. She said she was going to stay with her mom in the hospital. He gave her hope that Vasundhara would be better in a month and went away to perform his duty.

She was asked to pay money to get a room in the general ward. She went down to pay the money where they asked her the choice of room. She felt an individual room should be better, as she was going to stay with her mom throughout. From what the doctor said, she assumed that her mom would be discharged in a day or two.

She was given a room in the first floor which had a window facing the backyard. The founder of the hospital had taken care to leave plenty of space for trees and plants. May be he was a person who thought that doctors' can do more wonders with the support of Mother Nature.

There were huge trees—neem, flame of the forest, eucalyptus. There were Indian Laburnum trees too that looked so beautiful with flowers. The tree had another name also. It is called golden showers. Megha wondered how someone could give such an apt and beautiful name to that tree. There were some plants which had flowers of different colours. They were watering the garden with the treated waste water. She pulled open the curtain. The sun rays came into the room squeezing through the dense branches of the trees. The neem trees looked like they had all turned wise with white flowers covering their crowns. The flowers sent a pleasant fragrance everywhere. It was cool inside the room.

She went down to the ICU. The nurse was waiting for an attender to shift Vasundhara to the general ward. She too waited along with her. While waiting, she came to know that her name was Madhavi. Her wedding was fixed for the next week. She said that she was going on leave from that day. She was waiting for another nurse to relieve her. She looked happy. She was beautiful and her eyes were twinkling. Megha always thought that happiness can do wonders on the way we look. She wished her good luck.

Finally, the attenders arrived to shift Vasundhara to the ward. They took her upstairs to the room and put her mom on the bed. Her mom sat on the bed. Megha did not know, if her mom could walk and she did not want to try either, as she was afraid, it might aggravate the condition. She had bought a mineral water bottle, bread and some apples and bananas. She had taken some paper cups from the shop keeper. She poured water to offer her mom. She drank it. Megha asked her mom, if she needed anything. She did not wait for her reply. She gave a piece of banana in her mouth and watched her mom chew slowly and swallow it. When Megha offered her another piece, she turned her face away.

She slowly helped her mom to lie down in the bed, but, as if she was a spring, she got up. Megha pulled a chair near the bed. She held her mom's hand. She pulled it away from her, but kept gazing at her. Megha felt that her mom had become very weak in just two days. Megha had a lot of things to tell her mom so she started . . . . She started talking about her mom losing memory, about what had happened. She waited for some expression. There wasn't a small change. She kept gaping at her.

Then, Megha told about her visit to Bharathi's hospital. She spoke softly and slowly. Her mom watched her lips move, without batting her eyelids. Then as if she was tired, she stretched herself on the bed. She was sound asleep within moments. Megha got up, walked to the window to pull the curtains to make the room dark. Outside the window, she saw a crow trying to hop slowly. Its mom stood on a branch, just above the young one. The mother crow watched her with alert eyes. The young one got tired after a few steps and rested. It started cawing.

The caw was returned by the mother with a harsh caw. It looked, as if they were both having an interesting conversation. May be, she thought, the young one wanted to get back home. But, the mom chided her kid. The young one seemed adamant not to move.

The mother crow landed on the branch near its fledgling. The kid gave two sharp caws and saw its mom with pride, as if it had won the argument. The mom slowly pecked its head with her beak and started walking in ones and twos with its baby hopping behind her, sad and angry.

Megha enjoyed seeing them. It's the same with humans too. When the kids give up, it's the mom who tries to build confidence, by making them do what they feel impossible. Parental love and teachings are the same in every part of nature. The child always feels warmth in mother's embrace, no matter what her or his age is. Now, the young one had reached the ground, hopping from branch to branch with its mom.

She waited to see how the kid was going to climb up to its nest. As if it were a break, both mom and kid started having a chinwag. Another crow landed near them. The young one hopped to him and flapped its wings and started cawing.

The recently landed crow gave something from its beak to it. May be, it was an incentive to the young one for having learnt to walk. Then the papa crow turned around to mom and started nattering. May be they were having deep discussions about what the baby crow had accomplished.

The baby crow, happy with the gift of sweets or was it savoury in its mouth, was silent for a moment. Break over! Cawed mom giving loving pecks on the kiddies' tail and they started practising their lessons. Now with both the parents around, he hopped from ground to a nearby branch. He failed to reach it twice, but succeeded on the third jump. They started their way back to their home. It looked very beautiful to see the trio chatting and hopping.

A gentle knock on the door made her get back to her kingdom. She opened the door and was surprised to see Dr. Subramanian standing there. She did not expect him at that time of the day. His visit was due only in the evening.

He asked with his pleasant smile, if he had disturbed her. She realised that she was completely blocking the door way in the thought process.

She asked him to come in. He gave her two novels, "Brave new world" by Adolf Huxley and "Our trees still grow in Dehra" by Ruskin Bond. He said, "I had these two books in my room. I thought it will give you company, when your mom is asleep. Have you read these books Megha?". Megha replied, "No, I haven't read Ruskin Bond's books. I am not a fan of Ruskin. But I will read this book. Thank you." she smiled.

He said that they were all short stories and a bit autobiographical. He asked her about the authors she liked. The conversation went spinning around books, authors, poets and poems. She was surprised to know that he loved reading books, in the midst of such a busy schedule. She told about the beautiful trees that stood in the backyard. He had never had a chance of meeting or greeting them, he laughed.

She asked him to peep through the window, if he was interested. She thought that he will not; but he went to have a glance. He asked about the tree with the yellow flowers. "They are called golden showers" she continued with a pause "Aren't they more beautiful than gold?" He agreed. She said she remembered a poem by an author whose name she didn't remember. She gave a serious thought and said Henry something. He asked her to recite the lines. First she hesitated and then she went on

No idle gold—since this fine sun, my friend,
Is no mean miser, but doth freely spend.
No precious stones—since these green mornings show,
Without a charge, their pearls where'er I go.

No lifeless books—since birds with their sweet tongues
Will read aloud to me their happier songs.
No painted scenes—since clouds can change their skies
A hundred times a day to please my eyes.

He silently looked at her, amazed at the way she recited the lines. When she finished, he exclaimed, bowing to her," Wow! That's grand, madam. It's not surprising that your recitation is so good, because you are the great Vasundhara's daughter". She blushed. He told that the lines were really great. He said he was very poor in reading and appreciating poetry.

He checked his watch. He said," Oh, I need to get home. My mom and dad will be waiting for me. I thought of dropping in and giving the books on my way back home, but I think, I had overstayed, madam. "He said he had to do night shift duty that day and would be in the hospital around nine in the night. He asked her, if she wanted anything. He waved goodbye and asked her not to starve. "You can get your lunch served in the room, if you pay the person who will bring food for your mother."

She felt light and happy after talking to him. She remembered that it was long, since she has had such a long conversation with a man after Ramgopal. She heard her mom's voice inside her heart, "Don't generalise Megha, not all men are bad, darling." She told her mom that in these past two days she had come across very good men like Suryakumar, Subramanian, Shivashankar and the attenders who helped her a lot.

She opened Ruskin's book and started reading it. She was visited now and then by the nurses. It was nearing noon. The door opened and Muthu entered the room with a bag in her hand. She opened a knot she had tied in the corner of her saree which revealed a small paper packet. She opened it, saying that she had gone to the temple to pray for Vasundhara's speedy recovery. She applied the ashes first on Megha's forehead and then on Vasundhara's. She stood gazing at her boss for sometime murmuring something.

Then, Muthu took a small box, opened it, fished for a spoon in the bag, asking if Megha was hungry. Not waiting for an answer, she gave the box with sambar rice and beans sabji to her. Megha ate it with Muthu watching her eat with love and kindness. She placed a cup of water near her and sat on the end of the bed. When Megha asked her to sit on the chair, she refused saying that it was uncomfortable.

Muthu wanted to know everything about Vasundhara since morning, as she had learnt what happened the night before, from Nirmala. The attender brought food for Vasundhara. There weren't any diet restrictions for her, but liquid food should be easy for her swallow without much effort, so it was porridge and a soup. Megha asked Muthu, if she had taken anything. Muthu said that she would, after sometime, as she had had breakfast very late. Muthu opened the tray the attender had brought. There was some soup in a bowl along with some rice porridge. The porridge had some boiled vegetables in it. Muthu went near Vasundhara and tapped on her hands to wake her up. Vasundhara woke up after a few pats. She saw Muthu with alert eyes.

Muthu started talking to her. Megha was surprised at the way she was talking. She was telling Vasundhara about the temple she had gone to, the way she had to stand in the queue which took a long time, about Megha and Bharathi etc.. She asked Vasundhara to get up to have food, offering her help to get up. Vasundhara got up and sat. Muthu took the soup bowl and fed her, spoon after spoon, all the while talking, as she did, while working at home with Vasundhara around.

Vasundhara stopped eating, after taking half the bowl of soup, which was quiet an amount. She had refused to take more than two three spoons, when Megha had fed. "Amma, you have to eat well, if you want to get better." Muthu brought a mug of water. She took a towel from the bag, soaked it in water and wiped Vasundhara's mouth. She gave Vasundhara some water to drink. Mom saw Megha and again turned her glance towards Muthu who went on jabbering non-stop. It looked like everything was normal with Muthu and her mom sitting opposite to each other and Muthu talking.

Muthu told Megha to go home, as she had come prepared to stay with her master till she was discharged. Megha refused saying that she did not want to go home, as she won't get sleep nor will she have the heart to do any work with her mom in hospital. She asked Muthu to come the next day after ten in the morning, as she felt she would know by that time, when Vasundhara will be discharged. Once her mom would be back at home, Muthu could help her mom out in the morning, when Megha would be away to the college. Muthu agreed to go home, half heartedly. She turned to Vasundhara and complained against Megha for not eating, as she used to, when Megha was in school. She asked Megha to take a walk outside, breathe some fresh air and get back.

Megha walked around the gardens. She bought three cups of tea in the flask, Muthu had brought. She got some biscuits. On the way back, she peeped into the visitors' room to see, if she could find Shakti. She was reading some magazine, with her son sleeping on her lap. She walked up to her. Shakti was happy to see her. It felt as if she was waiting to converse with someone. She told her happily that her husband was getting well.

"The doctors are very positive now. I called my parents and in laws yesterday. They are on their way to see us. It has been seven years, since I met them. They have not seen my son too". Megha prayed for all happiness in Shakti's life. Shakti felt bad for not contacting their parents earlier, being afraid that they would never talk to her. Her fear was in a way justified, as they had tried meeting their parents after marriage and when she was in family way, but their parents did not want to do have any contact with them. Megha told her that her mom had taken some liquid diet. She bade her good luck and walked back to the room.

She met Deepa, the nurse who was in the ICU, when her mom got admitted. Deepa came along with her to the room, asking how her mom was doing. When Megha tried to push open the door, it was found to be locked inside. She knocked and waited. She heard Muthu's voice asking her to wait. She was puzzled. She could not guess what Muthu was up to. So she was surprised, when Muthu opened the door.

Vasundhara's hair was neatly combed. Her face was wiped clean and a new sticker bindi perched on her forehead, with the sacred ash on top. Her mom sat in the middle of the cot, turning the pages of the book Megha had left on the cot. When her mom heard Deepa and Megha enter the room, she turned her head towards them.

Deepa told Megha that her mom would recover soon as she was alert. Deepa talked for a few minutes and left. Megha asked Muthu to eat. But Muthu told her to eat the food, she had brought for dinner. She said that she would have food after going home. Megha gave her a cup of tea, banana and biscuits. She had them and left.

Megha sat with her mom. Megha decided to read out the book for her. She showed Vasundhara both the books, asking her to select the book, she wanted her to read. Megha decided on Ruskin, while Vasundhara saw both the books with a glint of fun like a kid. She placed the other book down and started reading it out for her. Her mom sat watching her face, while she read. She stopped in between, discussed and told her opinion, as she always did, when she read with her mom. When she stopped abruptly, to see her mom's reaction, her mom waited for sometime, seeing her face and then her glance went towards the book. It never left the book till Megha started reading.

Once again her glance rested on Megha's face, when she started reading. Megha made a mental note to tell Dr.Subramanian and ask him, if that meant she understood what she was reading. After an hour, her mom stretched herself on the bed and watched her read. Then she went to sleep. Megha closed the book. She was very exhausted and tired. She too stretched herself on the cot near her mom and dozed off.

It was four in the evening, when she woke up. She had slept for almost three hours. Her mother was still napping. She drank a cup of tea and waited for her mom to wake up. A young doctor came to check her mom. This was the first time, she was seeing him. When he held her mom's hand to check the pulse, Vasundhara woke up. He asked her, if she had any pain. He asked Megha, if she had taken anything. Megha told him that she had taken soup and some porridge. After the doctor left, she gave her milk, which she drank slowly. She dipped the biscuit in milk and gave her, which she ate.

Megha was happy that Vasundhara was taking something. Nirmala came to see her, stayed for some time, talked to Vasundhara amma and left. Megha started to read the novel. Vasundhara reacted the same way she did in the afternoon. Vasundhara ate a few pieces of idli and stretched on the bed with her eyes open. Megha had the food Muthu had brought for her.

Her mom saw Megha wash the boxes, drink water and sit near her. She started reading to her again. She was reading, when Dr. Subramanian knocked and opened the door. He never expected Megha to be reading to her mother. So, he watched her, amused. Megha told him about her mom's reaction to her reading. At first he dismissed it as her imagination, but when Megha showed him, he was surprised at her reaction. He told Megha that he was not sure, if she understood what she was reading or was just reacting, but he was happy that she was alert. After he left, Megha read out the book for some time, gave milk to her mom and made her sleep. Megha did not get sleep and so she kept chewing the cud about the events that had happened, till sleep invaded her eyes.

TIDE 13

Megha woke to the melody of birds. She had a good night's sleep. She did not wake up except twice to check on her mom. Her mom was still fast asleep. She checked her watch to know the time. It was five in the morning. She brushed her teeth and washed her face. She sat on the bed near her mom. She slowly stroked her mom's hair, face and held her hands. Mom was still fast asleep. She covered her mom with the bed sheet.

The screeching of the birds beckoned Megha to the window. She went to the window to have a glimpse at the world of Nature. All the trees housed a variety of birds. They talked and sang all at once. She saw two black birds that were perched on a neem tree very near the window practising to sing. They sang short notes at the beginning. One sang a note, while the other repeated. After sometime, the note became a bit longer.

There were a few mynahs, who were all dolled up with yellow mascara, discussing heatedly. One was screeching at the top of its voice, while the others, though, were loud couldn't reach that decibel. It looked like the MLAs having heated arguments in the assembly. May be they too were discussing something about their society.

The crow family that she saw yesterday was feeding the young one. They may get ready to walk their kid after the breakfast, she thought. There were a few woodpeckers, already on the job of building homes on the trees. Then, there were tree pies, singing a chorus with every step they took.

She saw two crows chasing a spotted bird. When it perched on the neem tree, Megha realised that it was a cuckoo. It shouted pathetically at every peck it got from the crows, whom it had thought were its parents. Megha saw the bird with sorrow. It's painful not to be loved. She wondered why God had created the cuckoo so lazy and why it did not have love towards its kids. Nature had made it that way. There should be some reason behind this, she thought. She laughed at herself at this thought. Human beings with their sixth sense abandon their kids in garbage bins, don't hesitate to kill them. Even her father did not harbour love towards them. He never visited them. When a man can behave this way how can she question nature's way of evolution? She saw the cuckoo walking behind the crows, even after it was pecked so harshly.

Seeing the sun's rays falling on her mom, she closed the curtains. Her mom was turning around and tossing in the bed with her eyes wide open. "Good morning, maa." Megha breezed to her. She wanted to get milk for her mom, but was scared of leaving her alone. Megha opened the door and peeped out to see, if she can find someone to help her. A few nurses were moving around from room to room visiting patients. A nurse who saw Megha told her that they would be coming to her room.

She decided to go out for getting the milk, when the nurse would be with her mother, as she did not know, when the hospital would provide her mom her breakfast and milk. Her mother got up on her own. She sat on the bed watching Megha. Megha asked her mom," How are you feeling, Ma?, Are you hungry? Do you want a glass of water, Amma?".

Megha's volley of questions hit the vacuum. She tried brushing her mom's teeth. She did not know how to make her spit the water out. Her mom swallowed the water. She had seen small kids do that. Now her mom was her child, a child who never cried, spoke or demanded anything.

The nurse came in wishing "Good morning" in a shrill voice. She was followed by two more nurses. Megha told the first nurse, "I think mom will be hungry. I will get her milk, when you are around. Can you please wait for a few minutes?"

The nurse told her," Madam, the attender will bring your mom everything. He should be here soon." The other two nurses gave her mom sponge bath. They checked her pulse, blood pressure and temperature. The nurse who entered the room first, supervised everything.

She called Megha," We are going to make your mom walk, Madam. Please come here and hold her hands. Muscles will get wasted, if she doesn't use her legs and hands for a long time. So we need to give her some physiotherapy", she continued, while making her mom stand. Vasundhara, once helped out of bed, stood upright, but did not know what to do. They both helped her walk. She walked with support, but was a bit wobbly due to weakness. After a few minutes of walk, she was made to sit.

The attender brought her, a glass of milk and bread slices. Megha gave her bread and milk. She, along with the nurse, tried making her mom hold the tumbler, but she didn't or couldn't, they weren't able to make out. The nurse asked her to make her mom walk for a few minutes, every four or five hours and then left. Megha felt very happy that her mom was able to walk, that she was getting better than what she was the earlier day, except for the memory loss. Overflowing with enthusiasm, Megha wanted to tell someone about her mom's walking session. With a gentle knock, Dr.Subramanian entered with a flask in his hand, exactly at the moment, Megha was eager to pass on her observations about her mom to someone.

She in all her eagerness did not allow him to talk, but went on telling how her mom walked. Subramanian watched her eyes, the way she talked, her innocence and the unmasked happiness, without interrupting. He had never considered about marriage, even though his parents had been pestering him for years. Now he knew that he had found his angel. He wanted her to be part of his life forever, if only Megha approved it.

Megha blushed, when she realised that she had been talking to a doctor who knew the condition of her mom. Subramanian smiled and assured Megha that her mom would start talking too in a few days. He asked her, "Did you have tea, Megha? I got you too a sandwich, as I knew that you wouldn't have taken anything." Seeing Vasundhara looking at them, the doctor turned to her, "Do you want some tea, Madam?". Dr. Subramanian told Megha, {Your mom will be discharged tomorrow. You can take her home. As she is medically fit, we do not have any treatment as such. She will get better soon. Don't worry. Keep talking to her. You can call me anytime you need me. Keep me updated with your mom's progress. Can I call you to know the situation, Megha?"

Megha wrote her phone number and address on a paper for him, requested him to pay a visit, whenever possible and thanked him for his concern and help. She returned Ruskin's book to him. He asked her to book an ambulance to take her mom home the next day. He chatted for some time and left. Muthu came around ten in the morning, as usual carrying a bag with boxes of lunch and dinner.

Megha started telling her about her mom, observing her reading, walking and being alert. Muthu too shared the happiness. She made Megha eat the breakfast, she had brought. She said, "I just ate a sandwich, Ma. I will have it later." Muthu took out the fresh sweet lime juice, she had brought and gave it to Vasundhara." She sat on the floor with difficulty, holding her master's leg and slowly massaging it. Vasundhara did not pull her leg off or react. After a few hours, Nirmala came to see how Vasundhara was doing. Nirmala and Megha went for a stroll for a while, leaving Muthu with her boss.

Some of Vasundhara's friends and hers came to visit Vasundhara. Muthu stayed with her that night. All the time they were discussing the ways to take care of her mother. Muthu wanted to stay with Vasundhara and do everything. She did not want Megha to appoint a nurse. She told that she would stay with Vasundhara, till Megha got home from the college.

Megha had no words to thank her, neither can she, for she was afraid of Muthu's ire. Muthu took the whole burden off her shoulders to hers, even before she could ask. She hugged Muthu. That's what mom always said that God sent some good people to shoulder, to give support and to love, when it's dark and full of worries. Sanskrit saying "Deivam Manushya Rupena" meaning, As God cannot come in person, he sends people as his representative when we are in trouble. She always said, "Remember Megha, be kind and helpful, be patient to sick and people in need for they are in distress and they need only hope and a moral support."

The day seemed to have passed quickly with visitors and with Nirmala and Muthu around. It was very inspiring and brought hope and confidence, when Doctor Subramanian spoke. She admired him for his simplicity. She called Bharathi's hospital to check about Bharathi. Everything was green on Bharathi's side. Muthu wanted to take samosas that Sunday, as promised. They decided to leave Nirmala with Vasundhara, when they went to see Bharathi. Both Muthu and Megha slept, after seeing Vasundhara slumber soundly, happily dreaming about getting Vasundhara back home.

The next day brought a lot of work for Megha. She got all the formalities done. It took three hours to finish them. She went to see Dr. Subramanian in his room to tell him that they would be leaving in another half an hour. He gave her all the confidence and told her not to worry. He promised to visit her once a week, to see how Vasundhara was progressing. She gave the other novel back. When she went back to the room, Muthu had already fed her mom, walked her and she was massaging her hands and talking to her.

Vasundhara looked at Megha, when she heard her voice. They waited for the attenders to take Vasundhara to the ambulance. They brought a wheel chair and took her to the ambulance. The attenders also helped her to get her mom into the house. She did not want to make her mother walk up the stairs and tire her. Megha made her mom sit in the chair in the living room, while Muthu made the bedroom ready for Vasundhara. They both walked her to the bedroom. Mom fell asleep as soon as she hit the bed.

Megha felt that it might be due to weakness, as she had not taken proper food for almost five days. Muthu spoke her thought by telling, "the travel would have made her tired, poor one!.You too take rest, Megha.". But, Megha wanted to bathe first. She had the lunch, Muthu had prepared and fell fast asleep. The exhaustion and tension relieved a bit with Muthu around and the hope that her mom will get back her memories, made her rest peacefully. Muthu decided to stay with Megha that night.

Megha called Bharathi's hospital and fixed an appointment for Sunday evening. The receptionist said that she would talk to the doctor and then confirm the next day. Their trip to see Bharathi on Sunday was confirmed the next day. Muthu was the happiest one. Megha opened Bharathi's cupboard. She searched for her laptop. She charged it and kept it ready to give it to her. She took two compact discs of her mom's inspirational talks and put them in the laptop bag.

Nirmala was to give company to Vasundhara. Muthu wanted to get potatoes and peas for making the samosas. So, she went to the vegetable shop nearby. Megha sat in the chair near the window and was reading, when the bell disturbed her. Muthu always took the key. She never rang the bell. Megha thought that she might have forgotten to take the key and opened the door expecting Muthu. But, she was rendered speechless on seeing Dr. Subramanian standing before her. She thought the doctor might have told her about his visiting her home, just to give her some courage. She never dreamt he would be visiting her truely.

He said, "I was getting back home from hospital. I wanted to see how your mom is doing?" He sat near her mom and checked her pulse. He asked Megha, "Is she eating properly? Is she walking and exercising her hands?". Megha replied," Muthu saw to it that my mom ate, walked and exercised". Muthu came in and welcomed the doctor. She told him her observations and got her doubts cleared on what diet she could give. She ran to the kitchen, prepared tea and gave it to him with some biscuits on a plate. The phone in the living room rang.

Megha excused herself and went to answer. He took the book, Megha had kept on the bed, when she entered into the bedroom with the doctor. He turned the pages and laid his eyes on the page where the bookmark stood. The book was Gitanjali, of Rabindranath Tagore. The lines that were there on the page, Dr.Subramanian felt, were echoing his feelings.

My eyes strayed far and wide before I shut them and said
"Here art thou!"
The song that I came to sing remains unsung to this day.
I have spent my days in stringing and unstringing my instrument
The time has not come true, the words have not been rightly set;
Only there is the agony of wishing in my heart.
The blossom has not opened;only the wind is sighing by.
I have not seen this face, nor have I listened to his voice;
Only I have heard his gentle footsteps from the road before my house.
The livelong day has passed in spreading his seat on the floor;
But the lamp has not been lit and I cannot ask him into my house
I live in the hope of meeting with him; but this meeting is not yet.

He hoped that Megha will also share the same feeling as his. He had met many girls in his college life and later as a doctor, but no one has touched and turned his heart as Megha. He never believed in Love and that too, love at first sight. Now, he stood a victim to that. He always called it nonsense, when his friends talked about falling in love. He felt it was just infatuation which will eventually fade off. He was surprised at the way she had invaded his heart and thoughts, on the day she had discussed about writers and poets with him. Megha came into the room uttering a sorry.

She told him that the call was from the Sanskrit college where her mom worked. They wanted to know how her mom was doing. Seeing the book in his hands, Megha asked "Ah doctor, do you like Tagore? It is the transliteration of Gitanjali. Have you read this book?" He said that he hadn't. She gave it to him to read. She said, "I love his poems. It's because the poems are woven in Indian atmosphere. I love Frost's and Keat's too, but I cannot relate to the situation in which they were written whereas with Tagore, it comes naturally". After Dr. Subramanian had left, Megha went on and on about the doctor to Muthu which made Muthu wonder whether the girl had given a special place for him in her heart.

TIDE 14

Megha found the routine a bit tough at first, but she got used to it within days, with the help of Muthu. It became a daily practise to call Ashraya hospital to enquire about Bharathi. Every day, she got up early around five in the morning. She filled water in the bowl in the garden for the birds and plucked a few flowers to offer to the Lord. These were the things her mom did as soon as she got up. Megha too did not want to leave the water bowl empty. So she continued the practise. She realised the peace that filled her heart, when she was close to nature at that time in the morning. She bathed and meditated for some time. She finished cooking and packed her lunch box. She completed all these work by seven. She then woke her mom up, brushed her teeth and gave her milk.

As she had to start for the college by eight, she gave the job of giving breakfast to her mom to Muthu. She had breakfast, dressed up and waited for Muthu. Muthu always arrived at quarter to eight. Megha saw to it that Muthu had no work other than attending on her mom. There was another domestic help who took care of washing vessels, sweeping and mopping the house. Muthu's duty started with giving breakfast to her mom. Megha returned from college around six in the evening. Muthu would have tea with Megha and leave for her house. Megha took care of her mom after that. Even after Megha insisting that Muthu need not cook dinner, Muthu continued to cook dinner. She even cut the vegetables for the next day. Muthu said that she did all these things, only when she had nothing to do, while Vasundhara was sleeping. Megha got so used to the system that she woke up even before the alarm went on.

Bharathi had completely regained her lost health. Megha had visited Bharathi twice, once along with Muthu to give the samosas and laptop and the second time to give her the books, she wanted. Every visit had a package of surprises for Megha, as Bharathi had become completely a new individual. Bharathi asked her about her mom. A lie that her mom would be away for a month saved her from further lies, but the way she asked every time made Megha think that her sister might have guessed that something was wrong with their mom.

Had she been the Bharathi she had known, she would have by now killed her with her questions and cross questions. But, this new Bharathi, was patient and calm. Almost a month had passed, since her mom was ill. Doctor Shivashankar wanted to discharge Bharathi, only after he had stopped some of the medicines. He also wanted to see how Bharathi reacted, when she comes to know of her mom's condition. He did not want to risk any relapse of the earlier condition, though he was 90% sure it won't happen.

When Bharathi had been afflicted with withdrawal symptoms, her mom thought it wasn't a serious problem. She thought a bit of counselling by a psychiatrist would get her back to normal. When she took her to Ashraya, Megha too went along with her. The doctor discussed a lot and he tried to make Bharathi talk. Later he decided to get her admitted as an in patient.

He called the sickness as 'PTSD'—post traumatic stress disorder. The name was a bit scary to hear. When Megha asked about it, Dr. Shivashankar explained, "It is an anxiety disorder that some people experience after seeing or living through a dangerous event. When in danger, it's natural to feel afraid. This fear triggers, in a split of a second, wild changes in the body to defend against any danger or to avoid it. This 'fight or flight' mechanism is a very healthy reaction to protect a person from harm, but in PTSD, the mechanism causes a permanent change or damage in a person. People who have PTSD may feel stressed or frightened, even when they're no longer in danger."

We generally don't know or understand many problems unless we face or experience them.

When Vasundhara wanted to know about who are generally prone to this disorder, the doctor continued, "Hmmm . . . . you see, brain is a complex organ. Each person's reaction to a similar situation is different. There is no age constraint to it. It occurs from a small child to an older person. Even war veterans and survivors of physical and sexual assault, abuse, accidents, disasters, and many other serious events experience PTSD.That doesn't mean that everyone with PTSD has been through a dangerous event. Some people get PTSD after a friend or family member experiences danger or are harmed. The sudden, unexpected death of a loved one can also trigger PTSD. The treatment mostly is psychotherapy and some medication. Being different, the treatment that may work for one person may not be good for another. So treatments too differ. But "psychotherapy" which is nothing but talk therapy is very important in these cases".

Megha was astonished by the way the brain, which we take for granted, functioned. The thing is that they were yet to know what really was the reason for Bharathi to get afflicted by PTSD. May be, Megha thought, the doctor would have known during the talking sessions and she doubted if he would ever tell them. Some things in life stay a secret forever and it is better that way. Megha was a bit apprehensive about telling their mom's condition to Bharathi. She was afraid of the after effects.

The Sundays, before her mom fell ill, used to be different. Megha and her mom used to starch the sarees on Sundays. Bharathi never liked sarees. She always wore salwars, jeans and tops. Bharathi did not participate in the kitchen activities too. She helped them by clearing the rooms of cobwebs, dusting the book shelves and washing clothes. Megha helped her mom in cooking. All the three went to market in the evening. They all enjoyed that time together. But, on these Sundays, with both of them missing, Megha, washed and starched her sarees and finished cooking in the morning by nine. She always ground batter for dosa-idli, in the evening and kept it ready for the week. After that she sat with her mom and read books or listened to music. She did not buy the vegetables on Sundays, as Muthu did it on Saturdays, after Megha returned from college. Sundays were the days when Megha took care of her mom completely, giving Muthu a break. She did not want to trouble Muthu, when she was free and around.

There was something else special about Sundays for Megha, other than chatting with her mom the whole day. Of late, she saw a change in herself, about which she was not clear, whether to be happy or scared. It was Dr. Subramanian's visits. The visits that started off as normal and usual ones, have slowly turned out to be special for her. She has started expecting him on Sundays and his calls daily. She enjoyed the time spent with him. He called almost every day, which in the initial days was to enquire about her mom, but nowadays went into other topics like society, their opinion on happenings in the world, about the new books released . . . .

The more she talked to him, the more she admired his gentleness, kindness, sincerity and humility. There was something positive in the way he talked and expressed. He slowly found a way into her heart without her permission and even without her knowing, when it happened. Muthu had told Nirmala about the visits of the doctor. Once when Nirmala called Megha on a Sunday, she told that the doctor had come to see her mom.

Nirmala teased her," I have never heard of Dr. Subramanian visiting patients personally Megha. Are you such a special person, dolly?" Megha's face turned red and she mumbled for words and replied," May be, he visits because I am your friend Nirmala . . . How do I know? I don't think I am in anyway special to him." While she said this, she wanted an honest answer herself.

"Ohhhh, Is it? As you have company now, I will come later. See you Megha." Megha did not know, if it was just friendship or more than that. She did not understand what and how she was drawn towards him. Whatever it was, she had high regards for this gentleman; she was happy and confident, when he was around and she missed him, when he failed to call. She did not know, if the doctor harboured the same feelings towards her. She felt he was just sympathetic towards her, as a fan of her mom and as Nirmala's friend.

Muthu had stocked the refrigerator with vegetables and fruits for a week. Being a Saturday, she came from college around three in the evening and relieved Muthu who went home early as her son was having a vacation for a week and was coming home from his college. Muthu's eldest son Kumaran was a very responsible boy. He was as studious as Nirmala, whereas her younger son did not have interest in studies. Nirmala was planning to put him in a diploma course after his 12th standard.

Dr. Subramanian called to enquire about her mom and to tell her that he won't be available for a week, as he was leaving for Delhi for a seminar. He said that he will be catching the early morning flight the next day and will be returning by next Sunday morning. Megha finished her dinner, after feeding her mom, and then cleaned up the kitchen. She played instrumental music in the audio player and listened, till her mom was asleep. The music penetrated into the silence of night, bringing peace to her heart and mind. She slept peacefully hoping her mom would get well soon and Bharathi will be back home to bring back the lost joy . . . .

THE BEAUTIFUL MIND

Born I was just like you,
Toddled I did just like you,
Prattled I too just like you,
Talked the way you did too.
I saw things different from you,
I saw letters talking unlike you,
I couldn't smile just like you,
I couldn't mingle as easy as you.
I am scared of people when you feel it enterprising
I am scared of sound when you feel it entertaining
I am scared of enclosures when you feel guarded
I am scared of myself and to be at home.
I have voices instructing me,
I have to abide don't you see.
I see people around me
always with me guiding me;
when I answer them
why do you laugh my friend?
I know you don't see what I see
or even hear what I hear,
Battling with voices,
battling with visions,
battling with thoughts
battling with reality
battling with myself
to live just like you.
One moment my friend
will you trade a day with me?
NO? . . . an hour will do . . .
for you to know my chaotic world
and will you help me win the battle dear friend?

TIDE 15

All human actions have one or more of the seven causes: chance, nature, compulsions, habit, reason, passion, desire.—Aristotle.

Megha started waking up early out of sheer compulsion and now it had become a habit. She opened her eyes and it was five minutes to five in the morning. Though she thought of sleeping for some more time, as it was Sunday, her system woke up, as it did on week days. She got up, brushed her teeth and walked to the garden. It had just stopped raining.

The morning still was dark and gloomy with dark clouds hanging everywhere, threatening to rain anytime. The sun was trying to send his bright rays to the earth, but lost the battle to the dense dark clouds. Usually she saw some sparrow like birds walking up to the water bowl to have a dip and a chat. But, today all the birds and bees have decided to laze in bed. The flowers were yet to bloom. They were waiting eagerly for the sun to show his grace. The buds were all wet and shiny.

There were some crows on the tree tops wiping their wet body with their beaks and by fluttering their wings. They looked at her funnily. A lonely cuckoo was singing loudly and sweetly piercing the silent morning, trying to wake up all its friends, who still were in bed. She too stopped after a few efforts, not being responded to her tunes.

It looked a serene and beautiful Sunday morn, though it was gloomy and dark. It started to drizzle. The cold drops fell on her slowly. She stayed there for a few minutes enjoying the touch by the droplets. Her thoughts went to the doctor, who told her that his flight will be leaving at six in the morning. He should be in the airport, along with other doctors, she thought.

With her thoughts flying to him, she walked to the kitchen, boiled milk, made coffee and sat near the window. She watched the rain that wasn't heavy and wondered why she always thought of the doctor. She wanted her heart to be honest. Why was she afraid to think that she was drawn towards him? No! Megha reprimanded herself on further thoughts about the doctor.

Mind . . . . it is very difficult to stop it from wandering with a simple NO!. Her thoughts went flying—"It is just friendship. Mani was a perfect gentleman. Her ideas matched with his and they could talk and discuss many things. That doesn't mean he or she holds some special feeling towards each other, does it?" Her mind asked Megha. She wanted it to be just a friendship. She thought, she cannot face another disappointment.

Her mind justified her interest . . . . "She had all the time been spinning around her mom, so when her mom fell sick, she was drawn towards this person who had the same qualities" . . . . it explained. She decided not to think of anything, about this relationship or the doctor anymore but her mind unconsciously expected that he would call after he reached Delhi. Megha stowed her thoughts away . . . "why should he, why would he?" She drove away her thoughts strongly, saying she had better things to do than brood over about the doctor. She was nearing 30 and was well past the stage of love and romance. It's very true to term the Mind, a monkey. If we fail to control it, it goes hay wire. It starts dominating ones thoughts and dictating with its opinion and wish.

As there was no sunshine, the job of adding starch to the cotton sarees was suspended. She took out the sarees, which she had starched last week and started ironing them one by one, listening to the music in the television. There were eight of them and she finished them in an hour. Breakfast was a simple affair on Sundays with two slices of bread or corn flakes or some fruits. They would have early lunch. She checked on her mom. She was still asleep.

Megha shampooed her long hair only on Sundays, as it took a long time to bathe and dry the hair. She came out with a towel wrapped on her hair. She started drying her hair. Her mom always did the drying part for her. Her hands ached, while she dried her long dense hair. One day when she was combing her hair, the doctor had come. He asked her how she managed to comb her long hair and keep it tangle free. She told him that she never had to do it until then, as her mom only took care of her hair. Now, she felt it painful to comb and dry. It almost took an hour for her, as she wasn't used to doing these things herself. She put a small clip on the top of her hair and left it loose to flow.

She saw her mom still asleep. So, she meditated with her mind running to the doctor, Bharathi, mom and back to doctor, his words, and a question that hung with doubt whether he will call or not. She wound up the so called meditation and went to wake her mom up. She slowly woke her mom up. She got up immediately, as if she was waiting for someone to wake her up. She fed her mom with cornflakes and milk, after she freshened her up. While she sat with her mom, she started talking, talking about

Bharathi first, then about the doctor and her feelings towards him and finally paused, after asking her what she thought about this.

Her mom was gazing at her, as if she wanted to tell her something, but couldn't. She slowly walked her mom and exercised her hands and legs. She helped her bathe and dress. Her mom never wore any night dress, but now she wore it throughout the day. She used to be always fresh and crisp with a cotton saree clinging on her. She took her to the pooja room, applied sacred ash on her forehead and walked her back to the bedroom. She always slept after these activities. She stretched herself on the be, but stayed awake. So Megha brought the brinjals and drumsticks to the bedroom and started cutting them talking to her all the while. She now consciously tried to avoid her conversation about the doctor. In spite of her control, she did talk about him, now and then. She decided to make drumstick sambar and brinjal curry. She wanted to make more sambar so that she can use it along with idli in the night. Her mom had started her slumber.

Megha went to the kitchen to finish off her cooking. She noticed her mom cough now and then, in the night and in the morning too. She thought that it might be due to the rain. She made a mental note to ask the doctor, when he called, whether she has to give any medicine, if the cough got worse. As of now, she decided to give her only warm water.

While cooking, she heard the loud sound of music from the nearby temple, wafting through the air into her ears. Oh, this loud speaker culture, she murmured. Once the cooking work was over, she went to check on her mom. She was sound asleep. So she settled down with a book near the window, seeing the hibiscus, the birds, the balance rain and gloomy sky. Her mind raced back to the doctor and she noted that she did miss him.

She could sense her loneliness, even with everyone around on that day, the day when Doctor Mani did not come, though she knew that he would not. It was nearing eleven in the morning. He would have reached Delhi by ten, she observed. She had expected him to call, but he didn't. May be he was busy with his friends. "Will he?" She asked herself.

He was being helpful to her, as she was Nirmala's friend. She checked the phone to see, if it was working. Then she cursed herself for being so stupid. Was she in love, she asked herself? She went to her mom's room. She sat near her and started telling her about the way she felt. She hoped her mom would give some reply, some help to know, what was that she felt inside her heart and whether it was right.

Megha remembered her telling Dr. Mani about the marriage that did not happen, when he asked her why she had not got married. Why would he ask such a question, if he was interested in her, she debated. When she threw the same question about his marriage, he said, he did not want to, as he hasn't yet met the girl of his heart. When she asked him to tell her what qualities he expected, he told her that he will tell sometime later.

She convinced herself that she missed him, because he had become a regular visitor and was a well wisher of her family. The phone bell made her run to it with expectations, but to her disappointment, it was from a friend of her mom. She wanted to know how her mom was doing and whether she could meet her mom that evening. Though Megha wasn't interested in talking to anyone, she agreed, as the person on the other side sounded genuinely concerned. She placed the phone down disappointedly. She was amused at her own behaviour.

There is a change—and I am poor;
Your love hath been, nor long ago,
A fountain at my fond heart's door,
Whose only business was to flow;
And flow it did; not taking heed
Of its own bounty, or my need.

She took a book to read, but her thoughts went racing back to him. She started reading out the book aloud to her mom, who was now fast asleep after her lunch, thinking that, that process would make her mind composed and drive away these thoughts. She read emptily. Not a single word entered her mind or did she feel she was reading.

She gave up this process, went back to the window and started watching the left over rain in the leaves. Brownie had gone away. The frogs were silent. The telephone again rang. This time, she decided not to expect the Doctor's call, but she could see that one corner of her heart was expecting it, even when she asked it to shut up.

It was Nirmala. She always went to villages to serve the people on Sundays. She had called to check, if everything was OK. Sensing a disinterest in Megha's voice, she wanted to know, if something was troubling her or if she was sick. Megha said she had no problems and was normal.

Nirmala ended the call saying that she will talk to her, once she was back from the village. Megha knew that Nirmala would now ask Muthu to check on her. She did not want to talk to anyone. She wanted to be alone and all by herself. When the phone rang again, she knew it wasn't from Mani and it was from Bharathi's hospital.

The doctor wanted to meet Megha on Monday afternoon. She fixed an appointment with him at two in the afternoon. She wanted to know the reason, but the receptionist did not know. She enquired about Bharathi and her health. The receptionist's reply made her feel happy.

Bharathi was loved by everyone, as she was there to help all. She was a patient listener that had brought many patients to talk to her. This was news to Megha. The Bharathi of past never had any patience. Her mom had always asked her to be patient, even scolded her many times for her haste. The receptionist said that Bharathi had become a regular part of the team, who went to villages to serve the people. Her mom would have been so happy to see Bharathi, in this new robe but unfortunately, she did not have the luck to know about these beautiful moments.

It was almost four hours, since she had fed her mom. So she made some milkshake with bananas and apple and took it to her mom. When she fed her, she told her about Bharathi, the way she had changed, the new friends she had made and the philosophy she talked. Her mind which stood in peace with the news of Bharathi, once again started flying towards Mani. She told her mom that Mani hadn't called. She felt tears peeping out of her eyes, but controlled them.

As expected, Muthu arrived around four in the evening. She asked Megha, if she was doing fine. Then she put her hand on her forehead to check, if she was running a fever. Seeing her red eyes, she wanted to know why she had wept. Megha changed the topic by telling about Bharathi. The phone rang again. Muthu waited for Megha to answer, but Megha did not move.

When Muthu moved to answer, Megha asked her to tell the caller that she wasn't available which surprised Muthu. She murmured," What has got into this girl within one day?" Muthu answered the phone with a loud "hallo". Megha listened keenly, when Muthu was telling about Vasundhara.

Muthu answered the questions that were asked by the caller. Muthu added, "a doctor", in between her answers which made Megha guess that the caller was Mani. Megha guessed that the caller was asking about Megha, when Muthu turned towards her, but told the caller that she would check, if she was awake. Megha came darting like an arrow released from the bow and whispered a hello in the receiver.

On the other side was of course Mani. She did not ask him, why he hadn't called in the afternoon, but Mani explained to her, his inability, by giving an account of what all he did from the time he alighted in Delhi, as if he owed her an explanation. Muthu, who observed the conversation, went into the kitchen smiling.

Megha's heart was now light and happy; she went to her mom and whispered that Mani had called and the gist of the conversation they had. Muthu, who stood watching Megha, teased her saying that she understood the reason for her behaviour now. She said that she would go home and tell Nirmala, not to come as she too wasn't needed. Megha reiterated that she was normal all the time and that Muthu was just imagining things.

Nirmala called to check up with Muthu. Muthu told Nirmala, eyeing Megha, that it took just one call from her friend, Mani, to make her jump and hop. Megha blushed and went away from that room. That call made her happy and peaceful. She went about her activities happily.

She had early dinner, as she had skipped lunch, after seeing off Muthu. She sat reading Keat's poems to her mother. Then gave her mom dinner and watched her mom having sound sleep. She thought of her helplessness in the morning and compared it to the peace and happiness at that moment. Elizabeth Barrette Browning lines . . .

> *There's nothing low in love,*
> *When love the lowest; meanest creatures*
> *Who love God, God accepts while loving so.*
> *And what I feel, across the inferior features*
> *Of what I am, doth flash itself and show*
> *How that great work of Love enhances Nature . . . .*

. . . . reverberating in her heart, she fell into a deep, peaceful sleep.

TIDE 16

Megha woke up fresh and happy. The enthusiasm she got after hearing the doctor's voice still lingered. The other reason for her happiness was that she was going to meet Bharathi. From what she heard, it was her guess, that her sister would be discharged soon. There wasn't a trace of dark clouds that loomed over the sky the day before. It looked bright blue and the sun was already on its job. Everything looked mystical.

She saw the sparrows were ready to have a dip and sip of water, with the crows, cuckoos screaming around. The flowers were all ready to bloom. The leaves still held tight, the droplets of rain in their leaves, unwilling to let go off them. After her usual morning routine, Megha cooked for Muthu and herself. She packed her lunch box and got ready for the college.

Muthu was always punctual and never made Megha wait. She came in and asked Megha, "So, what's the news, princess?, You look very bright and happy." Muthu wanted to prepare fresh dishes for Vasundhara. Breakfast was the only thing Megha prepared for her mom. Muthu prepared porridge, idli, dosa or curd rice for lunch, as Megha's mom ate them with ease.

Megha told Muthu, "Bharathi's doctor called. He wanted me to meet him at 2 in the afternoon. I guess that he is going to discharge Bharathi. So I will take half a day leave from the college and go to the hospital. After I see the doctor and Bharathi, I will get back home. I should be back before five in the evening". Muthu replied, "Don't worry Megha, it's okay even, if it gets late. I can go a bit late. Bring the good news about Bharathi's discharge. That's enough for me."

When she was about to leave for the college, Muthu came to the door, and told her," Be careful ", as she always did, when she went to school and college, and closed the door behind her.

Megha had two classes in the morning. She finished them, had lunch and started an hour after midday. It was hot with the sun sending its rays on everyone on the road. Development had seen a lot of trees being cut. So there wasn't a single tree to offer shade, when people walked on the road.

The footpath that is meant to be used by pedestrians, which was already narrow, had shops of all kinds with pools of people standing to see or buy things. Every time, the pedestrians had to get down from the platform and to climb up again, while speeding motorists and cars fled. They had eateries too on the footpath, the people who ate there washed their hands there itself. No one bothered about the people walking. Everyone was busy in his own world. It was a game of hide and seek between the government and shopkeepers to warn and remove the shops which reappeared after three days. The shopkeepers, Megha heard, paid to policemen, dadas of that area, the politicians etc. to keep themselves alive. So she hopped on and off, up and down the footpath and reached the bus stop.

There was a cart full of tender coconuts sold by a woman near the bus stop. Due to the heat, there were many, who wanted to drink coconut water. Rain made the atmosphere clear of dust. The sun was shining heartlessly making everyone fret and sweat. The nature's gift to beat heat—tender coconuts came in handy to everyone.

She saw the woman beautifully carving out the crown, making a hole in that hard shell and inserting a straw to drink. She did the job with such an ease and so artistically that Megha watched the way her sickle went on cutting the coconuts. The stray dogs licked the shells that were thrown and quenched their thirst with the few drops left in them. Her bus arrived with just a few passengers and a lot of seats. She sat on the one which did not face the sun. It took 40 minutes to reach the hospital and she was five minutes ahead of the appointment.

Megha was asked to wait in a room where there was none. She saw a blow up of a portrait of nature, beautifully painted and the wordings under went, "Just because you don't look like the other crayons in the box does not mean that you can't paint the most beautiful picture in the world. Don't ever give up on you". It was beautiful and inspiring. She hadn't seen it last time. Megha thought," Observing things also depends on the state of the mind." She went near and inspected the painting. It was written below that it was painted by one of the inmates.

She felt that the people with mental illness were true, honest, weren't selfish, never greedy, and they never teased the other person for their bizarre behaviour; but people who were termed normal had all vices, did not have the heart to hear or console or speak with these selfless people. In a way, she thought these special people were kept here to safe guard them from the truly mentally sick people, who are lurking outside and are very dangerous.

It was half past two, when Doctor Shivashankar called her in. He told her that Bharathi was improving very beautifully and there is nothing to fear about her. He told her, "I think, we can tell about your mom's condition to Bharathi, Megha. That is why I called you." Megha could sense fear grip her. She did not want Bharathi to get back into the shell again. The doctor was confident. He was so happy at the way she did all the work with perfection and dedication. He told Megha not to worry, as he knew that nothing can go wrong.

"I will be with you, when you tell her. So, don't get tense. "Asked if she was to talk to Bharathi today, he told her that Bharathi had gone out with the service team to a child care hospital, from where they had received a message about a kid with some mental aberration. Precisely at that moment, there was a knock at the door. When the doctor told "Come in", Bharathi breezed in, telling him that they had brought the kid there, as he had a lot of bruises. She did not even turn to see who else was present there.

The doctor turned her attention to Megha. Bharathi jumped with joy and hugged her. Megha gave her the nutties, the nuts covered with chocolate which Bharathi loved. She took it thanking her. She said that she would be using it, when she visited the village the next week. She asked the doctor permission to talk to Megha. He agreed. He asked Bharathi to take her sister to the garden where she can talk. Bharathi had to give the file she had, about the boy's sickness to the reception desk. She asked Megha to wait till she got back.

Doctor Shivashankar told Megha that the news can be given on Thursday. Today, she can just chat with her. He said that he had no fear about Bharathi, as she was perfectly normal. Megha too was extremely happy, seeing her sister back in her old spirits. She missed her mom very much. How happy she would have been, had she been here now!

Bharathi took Megha to the garden. She patted Megha and asked her what was troubling her. Megha answered in negative. She told Megha that she could make out the storm in Megha's mind from her eyes. Bharathi continued in her soft voice," I am not forcing you to tell me, why you look so tired and down. If you want me to know, I am sure, you won't keep it away from me. I will wait till you are ready to tell me. If it is about me that you are worrying about, I can tell you not to worry, Megha. I am completely normal and very happy, for I have found the purpose of my birth."

She went on, "Life always presents itself with struggles and troubles. These are given to make a person mature and strong. Your marriage was stopped, because destiny thought Ramgopal wasn't a match for you. We see the reason very late or never come to know at all. Everything in this world, Megha, ... happens with a reason". She paused for a moment.

Then she went on about their dad. She said, "it was good that he left us all. Otherwise, Mom couldn't have raised us so nicely. May be, our dad stays somewhere now, repenting for what he did or is still arrogant enjoying wealth and luxury. But, a day will come, when he will realise the wrongs, he had done."

Megha wanted to tell Bharathi that their father had come and that had led to many problems. But, she refrained with lot of difficulty. Bharathi fell silent for a few minutes, as if she was debating about something. Then she continued saying that she was happy that Megha had come alone. She started telling her about what had led to her depression.

She recollected, "That day, I had to meet a person in another office, where I was to discuss a project with him. The place was a few hours away from where I was staying and I had to take a train. From the station, I hired a cab. When I was travelling in the cab, the brake of another vehicle that was near mine failed. The driver couldn't control the vehicle and the vehicle started moving haphazardly. The car I was in, was missed being hit. Before we could all realise, the signal turned red and the pedestrians started crossing the road. This brakeless car, hit a mom and her kid in the pram who were crossing the road, killing them both instantly, while her other kid, who had not reached the spot, as she was a few paces away from her mom, escaped. The driver of the car too died after banging a lamp post, that was on the side of the road". She stopped, as if she was seeing the scene again and started, after a deep breath.

All these happened before my eyes and in the spur of a moment. Something cracked inside me, while the accident showed me how fragile life was. I was afraid of life and death; I did not understand the meaning of life. The three year old kid who stood weeping near her dead mom showed me that nothing can ever bring back the lady's life. I was confused, sad, frightened and sorry.

The accident kept flashing before me and I could do nothing to stop it. I asked the driver to drive me back to my apartment. I remember resigning my job immediately. I wanted to get back home to mom and wanted to talk to her. I never could get myself to talk or think until Suryakumar and Dr. Shivashankar talked to me. I told them about my fear and doubt.

Suryakumar gave me the Bhagavat Gita to read. I told him that I had never touched the book or listened to mom's lectures on it. But when I read it, I found that it was wonderful. I saw these people serving the weak. Everyone has a reason to be born. I wanted to live for a cause, ... I found out after I came here. I am happy that God made me realise the reason of my life, though after a lot of turmoil.

Earleir, I wanted to end my life, thinking that will be free from these troublesome thoughts. I never thought of the pain, I was to bring on mom, you and the people who loved me". Megha couldn't control herself, on hearing Bharathi speak. She broke down. Bharathi's voice choked now and then.

"Destiny wanted me to live, Megha, so God sent mom at the right time to save me" Bharathi declared, "for every individual has a reason to live on this earth."

"I saw people suffering here with many problems like depression, the way the bipolar inflicted suffered, the way schizophrenia afflicted people were left to the roads, my mind decided to serve them and help these people who are making their lives better".

Bharathi said that she has started applying for jobs. "Once I get a job, I will keep a small amount formy survival and the rest, I have decided to contribute to the hospital, doctor and Suryakumar are building". Bharathi finished.

Megha had no words to express her thoughts. She hugged and kissed her sister and said that she had made them proud. She told her," Bharathi, is an apt name for you and mom has chosen it beautifully. Bharathi, she named you, as she loved the principles of our Tamil poet, Bharathiyar. Poet Bharathiyar always wanted the women of his country to be strong, bold and to achieve."

Megha told Bharathi that their mom would be very proud to have her as daughter. Bharathi told her that she wanted to know more about Gita and other epics from her mom. She told her that she had failed to appreciate these values till she tasted it. She smiled and said, "Megha, is it not true that we always seem to miss the values of things, when they are near and easy to reach?" Megha agreed, but how will her darling sister react when she comes to know of their mom? "Oh, God", she begged, "Give my sister the courage to face the truth".

Bharathi shook Megha from her reverie. "So Megha, Whatever is bothering you, don't worry. It has come with a reason. It will go off just like the clouds that get dissipated by the winds. Whenever you want to tell me, you can, Megha. I will not force you." she said.

It was funny. Megha had come to see the patient, her sister and she tells her to be strong. She stood tall in her heart, in words and deeds and thoughts. She was very proud of her. Her heart felt light. She knew that Megha would be able to handle anything in this world with her little sister around.

It was Bharathi who again said that it was getting late and she should go back home. She asked her to convey her wishes to Muthu and Nirmala. Surprisingly, she did not ask Megha to tell her mother to call her, but asked her to convey her wishes and love. She also asked her to convey her mom that she was all ears to hear her mom recite from the epics.

Megha felt, as if she was in some other world, dreaming all these things, but they were all true. She kissed Bharathi and left. This time, she called an auto, as she wanted to tell her mom about Bharathi and Muthu too, who will be all ears to hear what had happened. Her mind kept echoing the words of Bharathi, one by one. She lived and relived each word, feeling excited, happy and proud of her sister, who had come out a beautiful butterfly, after passing through all the struggles needed for the transformation.

TIDE 17

Megha reached home, paid for the auto and climbed the steps in twos and threes. She always climbed the stairs in this pattern, whenever she felt extremely happy. She opened the door and surprised and scared Muthu with a hug and a jump. Muthu stood stupefied, not knowing what the matter was. This act wasn't new to her, Megha always acted this way, when she was excited. But it came as a surprise at this moment.

Actually she had started getting worried about Megha, as it was getting late. Even before Muthu could open her mouth, Megha took Muthu's hand and dragged her to her mom's room. She started telling everything from the time she went to the hospital up to the dialogue, she had had with Bharathi. Muthu was overwhelmed on hearing about the vast change in Bharathi. She thanked God. She told Vasundhara who was now awake due to the commotion caused by Megha, "Try to gather courage, Amma, get out of your trance and come out soon to see the fruit of the strife you underwent."

Muthu remembered something that had escaped her mind, because of Megha's excited entry. She brought a parcel and told her that it arrived in the afternoon. Megha checked to see to whom it was addressed. It was for her. She wondered who on the earth could have sent her the parcel. She couldn't think of anyone in particular. Curiosity invading her, she started opening the wrapper, when Muthu told her," Megha, Dr. Subramanian called twice. He wanted to talk to you. He said he will call you around nine in the night, after dinner." Megha saw the time, it was seven already. She asked Muthu, "Did he tell you what he wanted to talk?". Muthu smiled, "How do I know what you both talk every day?" and went away.

Megha's attention went to the parcel now. She inspected the parcel in her hand. Her name was printed on the brown paper that was wrapped around a box. It looked like a box, when she felt it. She opened it. It revealed a beautiful pink shining gift wrapper with small flowers in silver colour. It had a light pink card on which was written," I pray it's a yes!!!!", written in blue ink. She was puzzled on reading the line. She again got the doubt, if it was really for her.

She checked the address again, wondering why a yes should be uttered. Her name was written in bold letters. She became more curios. She opened the wrapper carefully. There was a box which had an envelope pinned on it. She checked to see, if she can find the name of the person who had sent the parcel. To her disappointment, there wasn't any. She opened the envelope which had a single paper in it. She opened it and saw the signature first. It was from Dr. Mani. Surprised she started reading the letter with a racing heart.

Dear Megha,

This parcel may bring you a big surprise. I had been debating for quite some time, whether to ask you or not, about the thoughts that had entered my mind. When I told my parents, they volunteered to ask you. But, then I wanted to be the first person to find out what you thought. I wasn't interested in marriage until I saw you. The more I talked to you, the more I was impressed by you, your goodness, kindness, the way you handled things, the childishness and the innocence—I can go on and on about the positive qualities in you".

She blushed and her heart started beating fast, when she read every word of it. "I am confident that I can give you a happy life. I want you as my life partner, if you agree and if you share the same feelings towards me. If I had disturbed you in any way by uttering something you disapprove, kindly forget this letter and let us be friends always. I will be waiting to hear from you.

"Expecting a yes!!!"

"Mani"

Muthu stood, in front of Megha, with steaming idlies. She had called Megha many times, but Megha was completely immersed in the letter. Megha wasn't on the earth at all. "Ohhh God!, when it rains, it justpours. It poured all bad a few months back and its all good today "she laughed, "if only mom gets out of her trance, it will be the best gift I can ever imagine" . . . .

Muthu looked amused, she said "Megha, you will be hungry, eat these and then see the parcel." Megha told Muthu, "Hmmm, I am not hungry, wait. I have some more to tell you . . . just be silent for a few minutes." She read the letter again. She opened the small package which had beautiful butterflies on a lavender background. It contained two books, one was "Pursuit for Happiness " . . . . and the other was "Love walked in", . . . "What a romantic way to propose!", she blushed and smiled.

What was she to tell, "A big yes? Wasn't she craving yesterday for the call? Didn't she share the same feelings as him? "She wanted to talk to her mom. Muthu had left the room seeing that Megha was too engrossed to be disturbed. She called Muthu, took the plate from her hands and made her sit near her mom. "What happened to you, Megha? Who has sent that parcel?". She asked her to wait for few more minutes.

Placing the plate in the floor, she took the letter out and read it aloud. Muthu watched her stupidly, as she couldn't understand even a single word. Megha translated every word in that letter in Tamil. Muthu's face brightened and she blurted, "Oh! is that why your doctor asked whether any parcel had arrived? Megha, what are you going to say? Say yes, you need a partner and Nirmala told me that he is a very nice person. What else do we need? Your mom will be very happy, Megha, say yes." Muthu was so happy that she ran to the kitchen and brought a spoon of sugar to feed her. She wished her that everything should turn good starting from this day.

Muthu asked her to have idlies, as she should have some strength, while talking to the Doctor. She told Vasundhara, "Amma, you have lot of jobs at hand. You cannot afford to be in this state. Get well soon." Megha couldn't eat the idlies. One doesn't feel hungry, when one is in extreme sorrow or extreme happiness. It's funny the way our system reacts to emotions. She felt inebriated. She was served an overdose of happiness all in one stroke. It was too much for her to take. She felt, as if she was in some fairy land, with fairies waving their magic wands for her.

She again glanced at the books and the read the letter again. Muthu called Nirmala in her hospital and gave her the good news. Muthu saw a glow in Megha's face. She thanked God for what was happening and prayed to him to make this happiness stay in that house forever. Muthu asked her to finish eating, as it was already quarter to nine. Megha gulped without knowing what she was eating. She drank the water offered by Muthu, again as if she was under a spell. She took the letter and the books, as if she did not want to part from them. She showed her mom the books.

Nirmala called and talked to Megha. She told her that the doctor was the best choice for her. Nirmala told her to take a good decision. She told, "Megha, let me disconnect. The king of your heart will be trying to reach you and I don't want the line to be engaged, darling." and hung up. The phone rang within seconds after she disconnected the phone. Megha had answered the doctor's call many times, but now she felt shy; her heart started beating fast.

She voiced a feeble" Hello". He too, she guessed, will be searching for words desperately, wanting to come to the point. He mumbled for words and told," I called you twice, when you had gone to see Bharathi. How is she doing?" She answered, "Bharathi is doing really great. I will tell you about our conversation, we had when you come here." She waited for him to talk. There was silence for a few seconds, then, he asked, "Megha, Did you get the parcel I sent you? Do you like it?". Megha answered with an hmmm. There was silence at the other end, waiting for Megha's response.

Megha did not know how to express her feeling. She finally found the courage and said, "I liked it." Mani told," That doesn't answer the question I asked, Megha. What is your answer? Will you marry me? I will keep you happy forever." She paused and said, "Thank you. The way you proposed was like a sweet poetry. I loved it". The doctor laughed with his tension relieved, "But Madam, give me the answer first".

Megha smiled, while answering, "Yes, I will marry you. But I want amma to get better first." He said, "Don't worry, Megha. She will get well soon. I am there. We all can live together. My parents will be happy to have your mom too with them." Tension having eased, they talked for a long time. He said that he was so happy and thanked her for accepting him. He said," I thank God for sending this sweet angel down my path." Megha smiled. He said that he would take her to meet his parents after he got back on Sunday. Muthu watched her throughout the conversation. It was in English and in Tamil. She couldn't understand most of it. From Megha's reactions, she knew that everything had gone well. That day proved to be a memorable day in her life

Megha and Muthu talked for a long time. Muthu slept, while Megha was talking as she was quite tired and exhausted. Megha couldn't sleep for a long time. Her thoughts went on reliving the contents of the letter. She remembered every word written on it. Finally when she fell asleep, the clock chimed twice to announce that it was going to dawn in another three hours.

It was six, when she woke up. She realised that she had overslept. Muthu had almost finished cooking, when she brushed and went into the kitchen. Muthu gave a peck on her cheeks, while she wished her a very good morning. Megha told her that she was to visit Bharathi in two days to break the news about her mother. Megha was confident that Bharathi would take it courageously, but still a bit of fear kept echoing in heart. She wished Mani had been around. It was very queer that nowadays she yearned for his support, when she was confused.

Muthu assured her, "Everything will be fine, Megha. It's the doctor's decision. He should be knowing better. The way Bharathi had talked to you, I don't see any problems. She will handle it maturely." True, Megha also thought so. But it still feels like a dream, the way Bharathi spoke and the maturity she had attained all of a sudden. Though she was elder, she wondered, if she had the maturity of seeing things like her younger sister. She doubted it.

She took the idlis and water to her mom's room. Her mom was putting her leg down and feeling the floor. She had been doing this for quite some time. It looked like she wanted to stand and walk on her own, but couldn't bring herself to do it. Now a days she walked to the washroom with their help. Once when Mani had come to visit them, they were both talking about her lectures. Megha played one of her lectures in which Vasundhara talked about work and fruit of work.

She had started the lecture as," Do your duty and leave the rest to HIM". Megha had heard it many times, but hadn't given a deep thought about it. But, when Mani said "it is a penance doing our duty without expecting the results. Somewhere in the corner of our hearts, we crave for the fruit, about what we will gain, whether it is worth doing the job or not". While talking, Vasundhara's eyes viewed them both and rested on the person who was conversing. First they thought, it was just a coincidence. But throughout the whole conversation, she sat and looked deeply, as if she understood each and every word that they discussed.

Megha made her eat the idlis. When she refused after a fourth piece, Megha tried forcing her saying, "Ma, you have to eat" and put her hand near her lips. That's when it happened. She pushed Megha's hand aside. Megha was astonished.

She called Muthu so loudly that Vasundhara got scared and Muthu came limping fast, nervous and scared. Megha told her what had happened. Muthu took the plate and gave Vasundhara a piece. This time she ate and then refused. When forced, she turned her face away. That was also a good development. She took the glass of water to her mouth so that she can drink. What happened looked like a magic to both Muthu and Megha.

Vasundhara slowly raised her hands and gripped the tumbler she was sipping. When they both looked in happiness and glee, watching the mother of two, a very intelligent woman, like a kid who was setting foot on the earth for the first time or uttering the first word in its own gibberish way, Nirmala arrived. She too watched her Vasundhara amma with so much joy and love. They waited to see what she would next. She did not know where to place the tumbler. So she saw them all helplessly with the tumbler in her hands. Nirmala took the tumbler from her hands.

Megha called her college to apply for a day's leave, as she was late and with so many things happening, she did not have the heart to leave her mom and go to the college. Megha, along with Muthu and Nirmala, sat near her mom. Nirmala was very eager to hear, what Megha had to tell her. Megha told Nirmala about Bharathi. Nirmala had tears of joy in her eyes. She wished she had been there with Megha to see Bharathi talk. Then she asked, "Is that all? Do you have anything more to tell me, darling? How is your doctor?" She told her everything.

Nirmala said that she had taken a very good decision. She showed her the letter. But, Nirmala told her that she never read personal letters and winked. Muthu told Nirmala innocently that there were books in the parcel. Nirmala chided her mom with love, "Oh amma, we should not read others' personal letter. We should not look into any other secrets of Madame Megha and the hero, Dr. Mani who stole Megha's heart, silently with everyone present. What a great invasion!" She opened her hands and gestured.

Megha turned away her face which had turned red. The phone ring brought them back to earth. Nirmala told Megha, "Will you talk to us, now that your Mani is calling you?" Of course it was Mani. He talked to her for a few seconds. He had called to tell her that his parents were very happy that she accepted him. He said that he was getting late for the seminar and disconnected. When she raised her face, it was Nirmala, who was readily waiting to tease her.

To free herself from the embarrassing moments, Megha changed the topic to "Bharathi". Nirmala offered to come with her to the hospital with Megha. Megha told, "We have to be there by ten in the morning. Dr. Shivashankar wants to be there with us, when the news is broken. As he has work after eleven, he wanted me to come there early. Though he was sure that Bharathi was strong enough to take it, he did not want to take chances. So we will start around half past eight, Nirmala. We will be there ahead of time."

Nirmala suggested, "We can tell her about Doctor Mani and you first, Megha, before we tell about amma." Megha refused. She wanted to tell Bharathi about her and Mani later. Megha told Nirmala "Doctor wants to take me to see his parents after he was back from Delhi. Can you also come with me, Nirmala? Can we take Bharathi too with the doctor's permission, if everything goes well on Thursday? I will be happy to take Muthu amma too, but someone has to stay with mom."

When Nirmala told her to take Bharathi and not her and Muthu, Megha told her that she considered her as her sister, like Bharathi. She said, "How can you talk like this Nirmala? Can my life be complete without you and Muthu?".

Nirmala told Megha with kindness, "Megha, let us face the fact. I don't know how the doctor's parents will react, with me and my mother around. Not everyone is as generous and as broad minded as our amma. So let us not complicate issues, Megha. I want you to be happy. I know that Doctor Mani is a gem. These small things like our closeness should not mess up your marriage. Try to understand, Megha."

Megha stammered, "No, Nirmala. I am not going without you or Muthu. I want people to accept me and my family for what we are. I know that Mani's parents will understand." From the way Mani had talked about his parents, she knew that they would surely understand and respect her thoughts. Nirmala told her that they could arrange a nurse to take care of Vasundhara for a few hours, when they all would be away. Nirmala was ready to do anything for the happiness of the family, she loved and worshipped.

TIDE 18

The day when Nirmala and Megha were to meet Bharathi, to break the news about their mom's illness, bloomed with mild showers. The rain, though mild, was washing the leaves and trees that were glistening in the dull, lazy rays of the sun. The street in which her house was located had the copper pod trees, standing proud, showing off their bright yellow flowers, flame of the forest trees with red blooms and the frangipani trees with their white flowers, spreading their fragrance throughout the avenue.

The contrast of yellow and red with white blooms, strewn here and there, along with the bright green leaves, looked strikingly beautiful. The flame tree really looked to be in flames with the red flowers all over the tree. The old flowers had fallen down, forming a carpet of red and yellow with some green and dried leaves. Nature always looked awesome, be it hot, scorching summer or fall, leaving the trees devoid of leaves or rainy season, when the flowers and trees look shining and gleaming with water on them. She looked up at the leaves holding tight a drop on their tips that was threatening to fall. A ladybird stood admiring herself using the pearl as her mirror.

When Megha was young, she and her friends enjoyed shaking the branches that stooped low, spraying the cool rain water all over them. Megha's heart was overflowing with joy that everything she saw had only smiles, glee and beauty writ on them. Though she had a small fear on a corner of her heart about Bharathi, the happiness she was experiencing, gave her the confidence and courage. Her instincts told her that everything was going to be great. When she told Mani about her fear about breaking the news, Mani responded positively. He told that the doctor wouldn't take chances, if he had felt that the patient wasn't ready to take in such news. He asked her to be bold and not to hesitate or lose her courage, while informing the state of her mom. He said, "Bharathi will get scared, if you weep, as it will lead to her conclude that something was terribly wrong with your mom." Megha prayed, before starting from home, for all the courage.

Muthu said that she had vowed to walk on fire in the temple festival which was to happen after three months. Tamil month of Aadi which coincides with August, had a lot of festivals for the Goddess Mariamman and her various avatars. The temples held this fire walk on one of the Fridays of that Tamil month. People fasted for two weeks before this occasion. They wore yellow dress, when they performed this walk. They first poured water on themselves, before they walked on the charcoal that's red hot, which was spread over a distance.

Learned people and atheists give a lot of theories regarding this. But it is performed by many, including children in many parts of India with faith and devotion. They believed that the fire won't hurt them, if done with pure devotion. They put the whole burden on God. That's what Hindu philosophy calls as "total surrender". When you surrender completely to God, He will see to it that you are taken care of. Its a difficult condition to practise, though it seems easy when told or we read. With our ego, arrogance and pride, its very difficult to follow this principle of surrender.

Na Dharma Nishthosmi Na Cha Atmavedi
Na BhaktimansTvat Charanaravinde /
Akinchanonanyagati Sharanyam
Tvat Padamoolam Sharanam Prapadye //

Oh Lord, I do not know Dharma, I do not know Dnyana, I do not have Bhakti in your divine Lotus Feet. I am Akinchan (one who does not have anything), and Ananyagati (One who is totally dependent ONLY on You). This akinchan and ananyagati soul is surrendered to your Lotus Feet.

There is a story in Mahabharata that talks about total surrender. When Pandavas lost Draupathi, their wife to Kauravas in the game of dice, Draupathi was dragged to the middle of the court. The brother of Duryodhana started stripping off her clothes in front of the court. She begged and pleaded the elders present in the court and her relatives to help her. But they stood silent. Draupathi just raised her hands and begged Lord Krishna to help her out of the situation. She did not bother to cover herself with her hands. Lord Krishna blessed her with clothes that kept growing, while Duryodhana's brother kept stripping. He grew tired and gave up in the end. That was called total surrender, wherein Draupathi was confident that her Lord will help her and trusted him.

Megha did not want Muthu to walk on fire, but Muthu was adamant that she would do that for everything to go well. A mother's love is very selfless and she cannot be stopped by anyone.

Megha's equation with God was different. She did not believe that God wanted people to commit these acts to prove their devotion. He is like our mother who gives the best to her kids; he is a friend to whom we can express our fears and happiness freely. He never punishes or does evil things to the people who offend him. If God behaves in business like terms like the people on earth, then he is no more God.

Seeing Megha silently walk beside her, Nirmala teased her asking, if she was day dreaming. Megha gawked and said that she was thinking about fire walking and what Muthu had told. Nirmala never wanted to criticise her mom's belief or stop her from doing something which, she believed, would please her and help her out of problems. She told Megha that faith is above any explanation just like Love. They came to the auto stand and bargained with an auto driver, who did not want to incur loss in his first trip. Nirmala asked him, if it was okay for him to start his day with a 'no' to his first customer and incur loss. That fellow gave a cold look and asked them to get in.

Muthu had packed breakfast and lunch for Bharathi. She had prepared the dish Bharathi loved and packed it for lunch. She packed extra quantities for Bharathi to share. She wanted them to inform her from the hospital itself, if Bharathi was coming with them which she believed Bharathi will surely do, after learning about her mom's sickness. Muthu can be amazing. Once when Megha was in school and was down with viral fever, she had to be absent from school for more than a week. Megha was in the sixth grade then. Megha wept for missing her lessons. Her mom told her that she would teach her those lessons, after she got better. But, Megha wasn't pacified. So her mom told her that she would get the notebooks from her classmates, after she got back from college. Megha did not eat properly that day. She wept even after her mom left for college.

She groused and griped about the lessons, she had missed, to Muthu. Muthu told her that she would help her somehow but on one condition. She asked her to eat the breakfast, lunch and medicines without giving her any problems. On that condition, Muthu told that she would get her the notebooks for her to write. Megha did not believe her till she promised her. So she was such a good girl that day, without making any fuss for eating and taking tablets.

Muthu left Megha, while she was asleep. When she returned, she had the notebooks and Nirmala was also with her. Muthu told, "What do I know about your class or books . . . so I took Nirmala with me to your school. We asked your class teacher and got all the books you needed. Megha, now be good and drink milk". Megha jumped with joy and hugged Muthu and Nirmala. She ran to the shelf and got her school bag. She spread all her notebooks over the bed. But, Muthu made her sit and read, while Nirmala wrote all the lessons for her. She did not want Megha to strain more, as she was having fever on and off. She never bothered about Nirmala, as she said that girls should learn to be tough, but she could never bear to see tears in the sisters' eyes or their mom. So it's no wonder, she had slogged so much with her painful legs and prepared all the delicacies.

Nirmala was positive that Bharthi will want to see mom and the doctor will permit her to visit home, while Megha had her own doubts. They thought of hiring a car, if Bharathi was permitted to visit home, as she had to be taken back to hospital after the visit. The big iron doors of the hospital opened a wee bit to let them in. The receptionist showed them the room to wait. Silence prevailed between them. Both were wondering what was to happen and Megha was wondering what the words she had to use to express her mom's health.

When they were both taken to Bharathi's room, she received them with happiness and joy. She asked Nirmala, "Eh! It is long, since we met. How are you Nirmala? How is your work going? I wanted to ask you a favour. Will you do it for me?"

Nirmala said, "I am at your service, Madam. May I know the type of help you may need?" Bharathi asked, "Can you spare three or four days in a month to examine and treat the people of the villages who don't have access to medical facilities?"

Nirmala agreed happily saying, "Command me, I am ready. I have promised Amma that I will serve the poor whenever time permitted me. I need to fulfil her wish and I know the state in which many villages are, without medical help." Nirmala told what her mentor, their mom, had told her that medical profession is a noble one. One has to do justice to it. Doctors should give confidence to a patient and understand their problems. She wanted Nirmala to be available, whenever needed unlike people who did this job just for money. Money is important, she had told Nirmala, but money is not everything. She wanted Nirmala to cater to the poor. Hearing this, Bharathi stated that they were all lucky to have a mom like Vasundhara.

Dr. Shivashankar breezed into the room with a good morning. He turned to Nirmala and asked, "How are you, doctor?" She smiled and said that she was doing very well. Then he asked Megha, "How is your mom's health?" Megha stammered, "She is getting better, doctor." She did not think that the conversation would start so abruptly.

Bharathi gave a puzzled look at Megha. She asked," Megha, when did mom return? Why didn't you tell me?

What's wrong with her? Why hasn't she come to see me? "She would have continued, if Dr. Shivashankar hadn't stopped," Cool, cool child. We will tell you. That's why we are here. Now sit down and listen calmly".

Shivashankar continued, "Bharathi, your mother hadn't gone to Mumbai. She was ill that's why she couldn't come to meet you. We did not want to disappoint you that's why we kept the truth away from you. Now that I know you can handle things beautifully, I asked Megha to tell you. Megha, tell her what happened." Megha kept telling herself to be calm and not to be jittery.

She started, taking a deep breath, "Mom got a shock attack Bharathi, a month and a half before. She couldn't identify herself or others. She was treated for a few days in a hospital. The doctor there said that it may take a day, week, month or even years to get her back to normal. There wasn't any treatment as such for this. But she is getting better. She couldn't grip a cup or drink on her own, but now she does it with ease. She still cannot recognise us, but I am sure, Bharathi, she will very soon." She stopped to see Bharathi's response.

The doctor and Nirmala were watching her keenly. Bharathi did not speak. She had her eyes closed. Megha was scared. She felt that it was a bad idea to tell about her mom at this time, when she was just recovering. Megha saw tears trickling down her sister's eyes. It was just a silence for a minute or two. But it looked like hours ticking by. Bharathi opened her eyes. Her eyes were glistening.

She saw Megha with affection in her eyes. "Megha!" Bharathi called, "Now I know the meaning of sadness that clouded your eyes. I am really sorry for not being there with you darling in this crisis. Poor one, you were left to handle many things single handed." "With Muthu and Nirmala doing most of the things "Megha smiled," I had no problem except that we all missed you, darling." Bharathi thanked Nirmala profusely. She stated "Muthu amma, is a priceless possession my family has got. She has it in her name." She continued, "Muthu means pearl. That too black pearls are expensive and rare. So is Muthu". "But, Megha, why did amma get a shock attack?"

Megha did not expect this question so soon. She did not know how to answer. Dr. Shivashankar told, "Tell her, Megha." She started, "Bharathi, our father came that day and abused mom. I don't know what happened to her, but she collapsed in the chair. She did not recognise anyone after that. The man came drunk and shabby. I still don't know the reason of his strutting in." Megha couldn't control herself. She started sobbing.

Bharathi knew that Megha was very soft and gentle in nature. She can never talk harshly or think bad of anyone. She was ready to forgive, even the man who had cheated her into marriage by not telling his ailment. She coaxed Megha. Bharathi told," Everything has a reason and our mom will be well soon Megha". Bharathi continued in a clear tone, "Life without troubles will never teach us its value and we will take everything for granted. With every trouble, we come out stronger and shining. We weep, as we don't know the reason and we always think that we are the most unfortunate ones. We fail to see the people below us, who have myriads of problem, yet live their life very confidently. So, Megha, lets not weep over mom's condition. But be happy that's she is getting better. Megha, do you remember, the poem of Henry David Thoreau"

Though all the fates should prove unkind,
Leave not your native land behind.
The ship, becalmed, at length stands still;
The steed must rest beneath the hill;
But swiftly still our fortunes pace
To find us out in every place.

"Don't worry, Megha, fortune will soon spot us and help us out".The doctors, Nirmala and Shivashankar were watching funnily at the turn of events. The person who was expected to break down was offering support to the person who was supposed to be strong. She turned to the doctor, "Will you permit me to see my mom, doctor?" The doctor replied, "Sure Bharathi, you can go. But you must return. I will stop the other two tablets you are taking by reducing the dosage in three or four days and then discharge you."

Mr. Suryakumar entered the room calling Bharathi. Seeing a crowd, "What happened?" he asked with worry soaked in his voice. Bharathi laughed," Nothing, my sister has come to see me. My mom is not well, Suryakumar. So I am going to see my mom."

Suryakumar told," I came to tell you that the project, we planned is really good. I was on my way to the orphanage we went last week, Bharathi, to check on the two kids whom we met. So I wanted to see, if you can come with me. What happened to your mom? When are you going?"

As if she became aware of the people around them just then, Bharathi introduced Megha and Nirmala to him. Dr. Shivashankar had a naughty smile, when he said, "Bharathi, will you please introduce me to Mr. Suryakumar who never has time to meet me after he met you. It looks as if the duo are everywhere together." and winked.

Bharathi chided the doctor, "Oh, No, Doctor, we go only after taking your permission." Megha watched Suryakumar who had shyness rubbed all over him. Suryakumar offered to take them all in his car, while Shivashankar coughed saying," Why won't you? "And Bharathi blushed. Megha asked the doctor and her sister, "Is there something cooking here that we have missed?." Bharathi cut in with a "No, nothing that I am aware of."

Nirmala asked them, "Do you all want to taste something really good?" and opened the boxes Muthu had packed." It was Bharathi's favourite rava dosa with potato stuffing. When they all took a piece each to taste, a nurse came in to say that a patient had turned a bit violent and had cut his hand.

Doctor washed his hand and told, "Bharathi, Take care and get back early." and rushed away. Bharathi told to no one in particular, "Dr.Shivashankar has a tough time with the inmates. Lot of patience and kindness is needed to treat them. Half the time he misses his breakfast, lunch sometimes even dinner." She told Megha," he stays in a room in the second floor so that he can attend to them, whenever needed. He is robbed of his sleep too . . . ." she paused. Suryakumar conceded citing that as the reason for patients improving quickly in his hands. They left a small package of food in the reception for the doctor to eat, when he got back.

They all left in Suryakumar's car. Bharathi was asking about mom and her treatment, when Nirmala chirped, "Bharathi, I have a very excellent news for you, but I need Megha's consent to tell you about it."

Bharathi nagged Megha, who was blushing and turning her face away from Bharathi. Nirmala who was very eager, broke it to her that the cloud (Megha) had fallen for the doctor who treated their mom. They could see Bharathi visibly happy. She hugged Megha and wished her all the best.

Then Megha told her, "the doctor proposed only yesterday". Bharathi wanted to meet the man who had captured her sister's heart. Megha promised to take her to him, after he returned from Delhi. Nirmala told her, "We all have to meet Dr.Mani's parents." Bharathi told Megha, "You wait and see, Megha, mom will become normal before your wedding."

Muthu had the door open, when they reached home. Muthu had a plate of aarthi which is a mixture of lime and turmeric, used to welcome new weds, people who return with laurels, who come after a long time of illness to drive away the evil eyes. Bharathi laughed saying," We are the evil people, who are going to disturb your peace, as we did when we were young".

Bharathi ran to see her mom. Her Mom was on her bed with her eyes shut. She sat near her, slowly touched her cheeks and called "Amma." Megha, Nirmala and Suryakumar stood away from the bed. Muthu was in the kitchen making coffee for them. Bharathi called her mother again. Vasundhara opened her eyes and got up. She sat on the bed and watched everyone with alert eyes.

She saw Bharathi. Bharathi hugged her mom and kissed her on her cheeks profusely. She held her tight in her embrace and started conversing with her. She told, "Amma, I am Bharathi. Talk to me, Ma. I need you" Megha noticed something different. She waited to confirm that it wasn't her imagination. She showed Nirmala, the movement she saw in Vasundhara's hands.

The hands slowly raised and hugged Bharathi. Nirmala came to face Bharathi and told her to stay that way and continue talking. Then she saw tears dropping one by one from her mom's eyes. Megha couldn't control herself. She stood before her mother, who raised her face and looked at her. She stretched one hand and held Megha's. Bharathi did the magic, Nirmala observed. She ran to the kitchen and brought Muthu to the bedroom.

Muthu stood spellbound on watching the things that were going on. Even in the morning when she fed Vasundhara, she didn't recognise, but she gripped the tumbler; she even held the plate for Muthu, when she fed her. They say when good time comes, it showers happiness and success. May be the good time started with Dr.Subramanian's letter.

Suryakumar watched the emotional exchange of the family. He had in his experience seen many people who had shown similar emotions, when their kids or siblings got better. Suryakumar had heard about Vasundhara, but he never had the opportunity to listen to her lectures. When Bharathi played her moms audio recordings, he also listened along with her. He felt that Bharathi had inherited that beautiful voice and the skill of oration from her mom.

He was surprised on the first day, when Bharathi talked to a twenty years old girl, who had attempted suicide. She was able to win her confidence and to find the reason behind her suicide. It was easy to treat her after that. The way she interacted brought Suryakumar closer to her. He stood awestruck at the way she handled things like a specialised psychiatrist. So one day when she told him that she never had kindness or service mindedness, but always thought money was the only thing that was essential for life and can buy happiness, till she saw a death and the orphaned girl, he couldn't believe her.

Bharathi freed Vaundhara from her embrace and sat on the bed near her. Vasundhara raised her hands and slowly wiped the tears in Bharathi's eyes. She patted her on her shoulders. She indicated with her hands asking Megha to sit beside her. When Megha sat down, she held Megha's hand.

Muthu came near her calling "Amma". She patted Muthu's hand. She turned around and saw Nirmala and called her near. Seeing Suryakumar, she gave a puzzled look. Bharathi introduced him. Bharathi told her everything about the doctor, the hospital, the project, her dream non-stop to her mom. Vasundhara saw her little girl all enthusiastic and excited, as she always had been and a bright glow, lighted up her face.

Bharathi said, "Mom, I will be back from hospital in three days. Then I will always be with you." She asked her mom to speak. She told them that she couldn't. Nirmala gave Vasundhara some water. Muthu suddenly remembered that she was preparing the coffee. She had to prepare again to serve it. She asked Bharathi and Suryakumar to have lunch and then leave.

Suryakumar did not want to disturb Bharathi. He asked her to stay home for some more time and return to hospital later. Bharathi told him that her mom would be happy, if she did something useful rather than just staying at home. They both had lunch. Bharathi bade goodbye and left with Suryakumar. Megha saw her mom wiping the tears from her eyes. She cupped Meghas face in her hands and saw it with love and affection. Nirmala pulled a chair near the bed, feeling happy to see her mentor back to normal.

What if she had lost her voice, her eyes expressed what she wanted to speak. With hopes that their mom will regain back the voice she lost, Nirmala and Megha sat gazing at mom in silence.

TIDE 19

Megha had jillions of things to tell her mom. She was at a loss for words, as she was very very happy to see her mom back to normal. She felt like she was up, up in the sky with happiness overflowing her heart.

Though Megha missed the honey dipped voice which had captured many hearts, she knew she will regain the power of speech soon. Nirmala was also silent watching mom.The silence among the trio existed for a few minutes and there went volumes of discussions.

Silence can speak volumes. You don't need words to express, when you meet a person after a long time or when you want to express something special. Megha asked about mom's speech to Nirmala. "Let's wait, Megha. She is getting better. She will get back her voice too. We will ask Dr. Subramanian, if Amma needs to take a speech therapy. Anyway you have a specialist at your beck and call and then what is your problem, madam?." Megha gave a big stare. Nirmala continued, "You want to tell amma about Doctor Mani or shall I?" Megha wanted to give the news herself.

Megha called," Amma, I have something to tell you". Her mom saw her wide eyed and she sat comfortably to hear what she was going to tell. Megha continued, "When you were sick, Dr. Subramanian, Nirmala's friend attended on you. He is such a kind hearted and great person. He came to visit you here, even after you were discharged." Nirmala watched silently, the way Megha was telling her mom.

Muthu entered the room bringing lunch for Vasundhara. She smiled at her boss and took a spoonful of sambar rice to feed her. Vasundhara took the spoon from Muthu and gestured to ask, if they all had taken lunch. Nirmala told, "Oh! Amma listen to what Megha has to tell. We will have lunch later. "She continued," She is telling about doctor. Wait till she finishes, ma."

Megha saw that both Muthu and Nirmala were so enthusiastic that she knew, if she paused even for a second, they will tell her mom about the proposal from Dr. Mani. When Megha was looking at Muthu, her mom patted her hands and asked her to continue. Megha continued, "The doctor is a neurosurgeon. He told me, amma, that you will get well soon, if I keep talking to you."

Nirmala interrupted "And Megha kept talking to the doctor instead of you, Amma." Megha asked her to stay silent for some time and continued . . . .

"He, Dr. Subramanian helped us a lot in the hospital. He visits us every Sunday to see how you are doing." Seeing Megha dragging the matter, Nirmala interrupted, "Megha are you going to tell or shall I?"

Megha gave in and asked Nirmala to continue. Nirmala told, "The doctor had proposed to Megha yesterday and she too accepted amma. They both like each other and he will make a good partner for Megha." Vasundhara smiled and gave a pat on Megha's cheek. Her face glowed bright in happiness. She indicated by sign language that she wanted to see the doctor, who stole her daughter's heart.

Megha said," He has gone to Delhi for a conference. He will be back on Sunday. He will surely come to see you, amma." Nirmala corrected, "to see you, Megha and not amma." Muthu watched in silence.

Muthu said after Megha finished, "See Megha, I told you my Goddess will bring happiness soon. She has granted what we wished, even before I fulfilled my vow." Megha had no comments. She did not want to make any. She bowed silently to the love of these women who held her tight, when she was crumbling down with stress and pain.

Vasundhara ate half of what was there in her plate and gestured that she was full. She gave the plate to Megha and had water. She looked tired and exhausted. Nirmala asked her to take rest, after giving her vitamin tablets. When Muthu adjusted the pillow, Vasundhara took her hands and kissed. This was the way she chose to thank Muthu who took care of her children, when she wasn't there. Muthu shed tears silently, holding Vasundhara's hands tightly. Then she wiped her tears and asked her boss to rest.

Nirmala left for hospital, after they all had lunch. Megha helped Muthu clear up the things in the kitchen and around. They both decided to nap, as the day was packed with activities and they were all exhausted with overdose of happiness. Muthu fell asleep, as soon as she lied down. Megha slept after sometime.

When Megha woke up, Muthu was sitting and watching her mom. She realised that she had slept for almost two hours. The time was four in the evening. Muthu removed the plaits on Megha's hair and started applying oil. She combed it slowly and gently. She always was proud to plait Megha's long hair. They both went to the garden and plucked the jasmine flowers that were spreading their fragrance everywhere. They both stringed them, sitting in the bedroom, talking all the time about Bharathi and Mani. Muthu clipped the flowers on Megha's hair. She turned Megha's face and kissed her on her cheeks and said, "You look like an angel."

Dr. Subramnian called her, after the seminar, around six in the evening. He was very eager to return. When Megha told her about Bharathi and the magic she did that day on amma, he was overjoyed. He was sure that Vasundhara's voice would recover too with time. He said that it can be decided after sometime whether she needed a therapist. He asked," Is she able to move around without assistance, Megha?".

Megha said, "She looks weak and tired. We did not allow her to do anything on her own. May be, we can try tomorrow." He asked," Now that Bharathi is fine, when will the doctor discharge her?"

Megha replied, "After stopping the medicines she is taking now, she will be discharged. The doctor said that it will not take more than four days. She will be here next week." He told her, "Megha, give all the tablets we are giving your mom. Don't stop anything. I will see her on Sunday."

After the call, she took the books and the letter to show her mom. Muthu had left for her house. As the food prepared for lunch was enough for them for dinner, she had no job. Megha asked her mom, who was awake and sitting on the cot with her legs down, "Do you want tea, amma?" She nodded her head. So Megha gave the books and letter to her mom and went to prepare tea for her.

Megha couldn't believe herself. She was surprised about the way life has taken a sudden turn and the way she had changed too. She had very strong conviction about not getting married. She did not want fall into another trap. And here was she swept by the love and kindness of the doctor.

She took the tea to her mom. Her mom was all smiles after reading the letter and seeing the books. She beckoned

Megha to tell her everything about the doctor. She was eager to see his parents.

Megha told, "He is the only son, amma. His father struggled a lot to come up in life. His mother assisted him and supported him, in whatever he did—be it charity or educating the poor kids. Amma, as a birthday gift, Mani's father used to take him to an orphanage or old age home and celebrated by having lunch with them. Mani told me amma, that his father wasn't rich, but he had a generous heart and his mom was a real "Annapoorni" who never could bear to see a person suffer from hunger." Her mom was happy.

Megha went to college the next two days. Sunday dawned in with excitements in Megha's heart. She was so eager to show Mani to her mom. She wanted to see her reactions on seeing him. She made coffee for both of them. Her mom smiled taking it from her. Megha whispered in her ears that the doctor was coming to check her health in the evening. Vasundhara smiled and expressed by waving her hands, whether it was to see Megha or her. Megha covered her face. Her mom came near her and patted her head. Megha was amused at the way this love, sweet love has changed her.

Megha told her mom, "Bharathi will be home on Tuesday". Her mom took the coffee tumblers to the kitchen. Megha watched her mom walk slowly. She walked behind her, afraid of her falling down. Megha made her mom sit in a chair near her in the kitchen, when she was preparing rava khichidi for breakfast. They both had it. She helped her mom bathe. The walking and sitting for a long time made her mom tired and sleepy.

Megha went with the books in her hand to the chair near the window. The only books that seemed to find place in her hands were the duet gifted by her Mani. The chair which had a soul as per Megha, made itself very comfortable for its heroine to sit and dream. She sat down with the books on her lap. She watched the trees, the hibiscus flowers that had bloomed and jasmines that were getting ready to bloom that evening. She searched for the brown coat bird that had interacted with her, but she was nowhere to be seen.

On a similar Sunday morning, two weeks back, she felt lonely and sad. Today too, she was alone, with her mom sleeping, but she did not feel the solitude. She was immensely happy that she even started singing. She read the titles again; "Pursuit for Happiness" and "Love walked in". It made her think, "Did he find his happiness, when his love walked into his heart?" She decided to ask him sometime later. She appreciated the way Mani had spelt out his mind. She breathed in the fresh breeze that came in slowly making her feel elated. She sat with her eyes closed thinking of nothing. It was bliss. She was awakened from the bliss by the doorbell.

She was surprised, as the time was just eleven in the morning and her sweetheart was expected only in the evening after four. Nirmala stood there beaming naughtily at the look on Megha's face. She had come to see Amma. She had skipped her service session that day. As she was fast asleep, they both prepared lunch in the kitchen, chatting, laughing, teasing and singing. It was like old times before Bharathi fell sick.

Nirmala and Megha never felt that they missed their father's love. Be it Muthu or Vasundhara, they both were great in their own way. Muthu's two sons respected her and loved. That way she was very lucky. She had seen many families where the sons too gave problems, along with the father. Muthu never pampered her children. They had to earn their meal. Megha thought of Bharathi. It would have been a mela, if she was around too.

They both went to the garden and plucked the jasmine buds in a bowl and stringed them talking about nothing in particular. When it was time for lunch, they woke up Amma and the three had lunch together. After lunch, Nirmala gave a pen and paper to Vasundhara and asked her to try writing. Her hands shivered and were weak. She couldn't and she gave up. Nirmala gave exercise to her hands slowly massaging it, closing the palms and stretching them.

The time raced fast, announcing them, it was three. So Nirmala asked Megha to comb her hair and get ready to receive the prince. Nirmala combed Vasundhara's hair by applying oil. She was talking to her about her hospital routines and the patients, while Megha was busy beautifying herself.

She came bedecked, like Goddess Lakshmi in a green cotton saree with a thin brocade of silver and gold thread adorning the ends of the saree. She wore nothing special on her face, just a small bindi, that looked beautiful and proud having perched on her forehead. She wore four thin green glass bangles on one hand and a watch on the other. Her ears gave space to the small studs which she had been wearing for years. Any attempt to make her change the studs always ended in failure. Her eyes had a thin kajal lining. Nirmala was reminded of a poem of Tennyson, which she had read, when she was in eighth grade . . . .

It is no wonder said the Lords
She is more beautiful than words can say
As shines the moon in clouded skies

Megha stood before them and asked childishly to her mom and Nirmala, how she looked. Nirmala teased her saying that she would have kidnapped her, had she been a man. But now she was sure that her prince was going to carry her off, the moment he sets his eyes on her. The bell announced the arrival of Megha's beloved, but she wanted Nirmala to answer the door. Nirmala refused. When the door opened, Megha stood before Mani in all beauty that all the words in the dictionary weren't sufficient to express.

They both stood face to face
Their eyes spoke what words couldn't
He opened his eyes and locked her in
She opened her heart and welcomed him

Vasundhara held on to Nirmala and came walking to receive her future son in law. She was curious to see how he looked and how he was. Nirmala coughed and brought them both to the earth. Seeing Vasundhara, he folded his hands in respect. He asked her to sit comfortably. He checked her hands, leg movements, her blood pressure, and her eyes and was happy that everything was normal. Megha went in to make coffee. Nirmala followed her. Mani talked about his parents, his profession and finally promised that he will keep Megha happy forever.

When Megha came in with coffee, he told her that his parents would come there on Wednesday, as they considered it auspicious. He said, "We don't want your mom to strain unnecessarily." Megha was silent throughout, except for a few words which she was compelled to answer. Vasundhara was very pleased with him. When he left, Megha went down to his car to see him off.

He said, "Megha, you look beautiful." She shyly told that she was very lucky to have him. They both talked for some time, while the copper pod tree sent golden showers of yellow flowers on them, with every sway of wind blessing their friend, who was the only one to appreciate their beauty, while the rest who lived in that street, did not find time even to look up.

Megha asked her mom about Mani. Her Mom showed signs to indicate that he liked the choice. Then the topic turned to Bharathi. She sat with her mom talking about the way Bharathi talked. Her mom's face was bright and happy. After dinner, they both listened to Ashtapathi, which is Jayadev's composition on Lord Krishna, rendered by M.L. Vasanthakumari. It is about Radha and Krishna's eternal love. She loved the second song that tells about Radha

lalita lavanga latA pariSeelana kOmala malaya sameerE
madhukara nikara karambita kOkila koojita kunja kuTeerE
viharati haririha sarasa vasantE nrutyati
yuvati janEna samam sakhi virahi janasya durantE.

Which means—Oh dear friend Radha, cool breeze of spring season from clove bushes is gently blowing. Cuckoos are cooing sweetly. Bowers and cottages are echoing with humming sound of bees. Sri Krishna is strolling and dancing with Gopikas delightfully. Come on, let's go there as we are pining in love for him."

Ashtapathi always brought peace and make us sense the inner beauty, when heard in the silence of night.

People have a wrong belief that Lord Krishna went around romancing with many girls. It is not right. The love between Lord Krishna and Gopikas is eternal. It's not lust or physical. It shows the immense devotion that helps one (jeevatma) to unite with supreme power, the Paramatma. Normal people interpret it as physical pleasure, romance and damage the beauty of text and the meaning in it. After hearing three renditions, they both slept peacefully.

TIDE 20

The day blossomed with golden sunshine waking up all the creations on earth. The birds were screeching a welcome note to the rays that came to wake them up. The milkman had left the packets outside the door in the bag she had hung on the latch. The bag had been used since long and so, one of the ears of the bag fell apart, asking for it to be changed. When we human beings need a change in life, why shouldn't these non-living things, which had been serving without any returns, revolt by slowly tearing themselves apart. She opened the packet, poured the milk in a vessel and left it on the stove to boil.

Her mom was up too. She had started moving around slowly. Mani said that she would be devoid of weakness in a few days He wanted to take Megha's mom to a speech therapist.

Megha asked, "Amma, are you hungry? Shall I prepare something for breakfast?" Her mother gestured that she will eat with Bharathi. So both of them had a couple of biscuits with coffee.

Megha cooked, whilst her mom sat watching her. Her mom tried to help her by dicing the vegetables, but she couldn't. Megha told her, "Ma, you can do it, after you become stronger. Don't worry" and finished all the work, by the time Muthu arrived, asking Megha, when she was going to bring Bharathi. Megha replied, "No ma, I am not going. Bharathi said that she would come on her own". Muthu smiled, "Bharathi has become the same old Bharathi who wants to do things on her own."

All the three of them waited for Bharathi to arrive. She came not, as Megha expected, in an auto, but in a car with Suryakumar. The words of Dr. Shivashankar echoed in her ears that brought smile to her face. But, she did not want to say anything at that moment. She told about Bharathi coming with Suryakumar to Nirmala the earlier day and they both laughed thinking about Shivashankar's comments.

She laughed saying," Two brides getting ready for marriage". It always led to the question, if a boy and girl cannot be friends. But, Megha's opinion was that we can have many friends. But a person gets into our heart, when we feel them a perfect match to us. He can be still be a friend because a husband has to be a friend too. Without friendship, there cannot be a good relationship between life partners.

Megha thought, "May be they were wrong. Maybe she was just being friendly with him". Megha had seen Bharathi with Suryakumar twice, but she never felt anything different, not until Doctor Shivashankar made that comment. May be the doctor was just making fun.

Suryakumar's parents lived in Bangalore. He had two brothers who were well settled in the computer field. They were both abroad. He had a sister who was a gynaecologist and was married to a heart surgeon. She had a daughter and a son. His parents were happy with all their children except Suryakumar. They thought that he was wasting his life.

Bharathi told her all these things, when during their last meeting. Megha felt that she would be happy even, if it was pure friendship or friendship turned love. Everyone loved Suryakumar for the way he conducted himself. He was so humble and down to earth.

Suryakumar had lunch with them and left. After lunch, Megha left Bharathi and Muthu with her mom and started for the college. She walked freely and happily, without any worry lurching her—after so many days.

Bharathi had started applying for jobs, even when she was in hospital. She had two interviews scheduled next week. She was all eager to get back to work. Bharathi sat reading her mom's book and listening to her lectures from CDs along with mom. Her mom watched her, amused at the way she had changed.

Wednesday came visiting in all grandeur. Doctor and his parents were to visit them after four in the evening. Megha took half a day leave and was back home by two o clock in the afternoon. She entered the house that smelt of goodies and had a mixture of ghee, sugar and cardamom smell wafting in the air.

Megha sat chatting with her mom, who was in kitchen supervising, Muthu and Bharathi who tasted all the things prepared. Her mom showed the clock. It was nearing three. So Megha got up, washed her face and got all dolled up for the doctor and his parents in a maroon cotton saree that had a thin jari border. The pallu was beautifully embroidered with golden threads. Her mom had got it two years ago, for her birthday.The family had a principle not to wear silk sarees. She followed it strictly, after she read that approximately 10000 silkworms were killed to make a silk saree. She felt bad about killing the worms to beautify oneself.

The family had great devotion on the Mahaswami of Kanchipuram, who preached his disciples not to use silk as it is made by killing silkworms. Yet another reason was that silk being very expensive, everyone can't afford it. She felt both the reasons are true. He also requested people not to waste money by lavishly spending in celebrating the marriages with pomp and show, but instead to use the money for financing the marriage of a poor girl for whom marriage is a distant dream for want of money. He also blames those who live a luxurious life, of tempting all others also to live like them.

Ramgopal's parents had wanted her to wear silk sarees on the wedding day and she had to give in, as her mom told her that she could start following her principles, after her marriage. She wanted to tell Mani beforehand about her principles. She was confident that he would understand. She wore maroon stoned studs and the maroon stone bangles that her mom had got for her from Hyderabad. Seeing her, all the three women felt that she looked lovely.

Bharathi helped Megha in plaiting her hair. Megha observed that Bharathi was talking a lot about Suryakumar. Muthu smiled at Megha whenever the conversation went around Suryakumar. Muthu had got her jasmine flowers stringed from market, as she felt there won't be time to pluck the flowers from the garden. She adorned Megha's hair with it. Bharathi always fought with her mom, when she was young, about her hair being shorter than Megha. When Bharathi looked at the hair after adorning it with flowers, she felt that it looked like a dark sky which had a cluster of stars in one corner. Nirmala had promised to join them after the morning shift. She was expected anytime.

Muthu asked Bharathi to wash her face and wear something good. She spoke the mind of Vasundhara. Bharathi wore a purple salwar. She looked healthy and cheerful. Nirmala came wearing a white cotton salwar with blue flowers strewn everywhere. She had come straight from hospital. Vasundhara asked her to change her dress. So she changed into one of the sarees of Megha's, while Bharathi complained about the length and other difficulties in wearing a saree.

All the eyes stood eager to receive Dr.Subramanian and his parents. Doctor, with his parents, was there by at half past four. Mani's parents were very simple. They were greeted by everyone. Mani's parents told Vasundhara that they were her fans. Mani introduced Nirmala, Bharathi and Muthu to his parents, while Muthu shyed away into the kitchen after serving them with water.

He called Megha and introduced her to his parents saying "My queen". Megha blushed, her cheeks turning red trying to match the studs she wore. His mom made her sit near her and said, "Megha, We are all very happy to welcome you to our house. We have heard a lot about you from Mani. We had been trying to convince him to get married. But, you made it happen. I have got a saree for you, Megha. Will you please wear this and come?" She gave a packet.

Megha took it and felt bad that she hadn't told Mani earlier about her principle of not wearing silk. She cannot tell them now, as she did not want to hurt those nice sweet souls. When she opened the packet, she was overjoyed to see a crisp Bengal cotton saree in mustard colour with a dark red border that was very grand. She wore it wholeheartedly. She was very happy that she was getting married to a family whose ideas synchronised with her ideas and feelings. She looked like a golden girl in the mustard saree she wore. They all talked about the date of marriage.

It was fixed after the harvest festival, Pongal, on January 26th. Both the families decided on a simple marriage function in the registrar office and after the marriage, they decided on a luncheon in an orphanage. They also would arrange a simple dinner party to selected people, who knew them very well, o announce the marriage of Megha and Mani. Megha pinched herself to check, if the happenings were real. She felt herself lucky for getting such good people. She remembered what her mom had told about all men not being cruel and wicked. Vasundara was very much happy with the marriage arrangement. Muthu called Megha and asked her to serve the delicacies prepared. Megha, teased by Bharathi and Nirmala, took the plates one by one.

Mani's dad asked Bharathi about her marriage. He said, "If you have someone in mind spell it out girl, we can have both the marriages on the same day." She told him," I will get married, after the construction of the hospital is over." "Bharathi, you can get married and still help in the construction of hospital too. We can find you a suitable match who will agree to all your conditions." said Mani's mom.

Bharathi said, "Not now aunty." When Mani's mom and dad turned to Nirmala and asked, "What about you, doctor? Aren't you also of Megha's age?". Immediately, Mani blurted out, "the groom is waiting for her to say a yes". It was real news. Bharathi started nagging her. Megha gave a surprised look. As Mani told this in English, Muthu did not get it. But she understood that it was something about her daughter. Finally Mani told, Nirmala's senior Ganesan, who is also a close friend of mine, is the man of her choice. He is working in a village, not worried about money. His aim is to serve the poor." Bharathi was asking about all the details. Mani told that he knew Nirmala only through him. Megha asked her softly, "Oh, that's why you go absconding on Sundays . . . you kept the secret away from me, Nirmala . . . too bad."

When Bharathi told Muthu about Nirmala, she told "She is a matured individual and very responsible girl. Whatever she decides is fine with me". But Muthu wanted Nirmala to get married soon. She told her that she can take care of herself and her sons too can manage their lives on their own. But, Nirmala wanted to get married only, after her brother got a job. "I will like to wait for a year for my brother to get placement" She said.

Mani and his parents left, saying that they would come another day to meet Vasundhara. After they left, it was chatter, chatter about Mani and his family. They chided Nirmala for not telling them anything. Nirmala smiled. Bharathi said, "I know now why you went to a village to serve". She wanted to know, if that was the village that housed the doctor. They all wanted to see him.

Nirmala promised to bring him that Sunday. They could see tears in Muthu's eyes. They weren't tears of sorrow, but of happiness. She held Vasundhara's hand and thanked her for making her daughter so good and learned. She thanked her for making her life that had been in shatters into a beautiful island. They could understand Muthu's happiness. Nirmala was the first person to be educated in their family. They had dinner, and chatted till daybreak not feeling tired or sleepy.

TIDE 21

The house of Vasundharas' wore a festive look. Vasundhara's health got better as days slipped by, though she didn't get back the voice she lost. She could speak in whispers and a few words in feeble tone. The whole house waited eagerly to see Nirmala's beloved. Nirmala brought her sweet heart, Ganesan on Sunday.

Muthu was so happy to see Ganesan. He talked to Muthu without any inhibitions. Nirmala reiterated that she would marry only after her brother got a job. Ganesan said, "I don't have any problem to take care of your family. Nirmala, you decide what you want. As for me, I am ready to marry you even now."

When Muthu heard these words from Ganesan, she told Nirmala, "You have done enough and the boys can take care of themselves. You get married, as I don't want you to make this young man wait any more". Megha and Bharathi told Nirmala, "You are being asked diplomatically to get out of your house, Nirmala. You don't have a place there." Vasundhara too asked Nirmala to get married.

Finally Nirmala decided to give in. Ganesan made a big bow and said, "Thank you all for making this marriage possible. I had been begging my queen to marry me soon." It was decided to hold the wedding of Nirmala and Ganesan on the same day as Megha's. Vasundhara was happy with her decision. Muthu wanted to meet Ganesan's parents to talk about the marriage.

Dr. Ganesan said, "I lost my mom, when I was very young. My dad too passed away in a few years. My uncle who was very poor, decided to put me in an Ashram in Madurai which housed orphans and the children whose parents who could not provide them food or education. The orphanage ran a primary school. For secondary education, we were sent to a school nearby which was owned by a philanthropist, who gave the kids of the ashram, free education.

"I was five, when I was sent there. My uncle did not want me to starve along with him. When I scored a 490/500 in my tenth standard; an officer in the Ashram showed my mark sheet to a donor who had come to feed us on his birthday. He decided to sponsor my education. He helped me finish my MBBS."

He paused and then said, "Aunty, I have got a mother now. After getting my marriage registered, I will take Nirmala with me to Madurai, to get the blessings from my mentor, who is now ninety years old, and the people of Ashram who made my life colourful". He continued, "I don't go to temples, aunty, for I see God in the smiles of the poor. My hospital is my temple and my God appears before me daily, inspiring me to do more service." Muthu was very proud of her son in law. She was confident that he would value Nirmala and she would lead very respectable life.

There were just six months for Megha and Nirmala's wedding. Muthu was to fire walk in fifteen days. Speech therapy improved Vasundhara's ability to speak a bit. She regained all her strength and had started her daily routine. Megha made her write a page and she was able to write better though not as fast as she used to. The professors and the director of the college came to meet her. Vasundhara did not want to be a liability to the students and faculty. So she wanted to quit the job. But, the college authorities were ready to wait for a few more months. Vasundhara wrote down in a paper and showed them that she would join as soon as she got well. She would work for her satisfaction and not for money.

Bharathi joined her job on the first of August. She was very happy with her work and went to serve with Suryakumar whenever she found herself free. She now sat with her mom for hours reading out the epics, listening to the songs and lectures of her mom. Megha was happy that the things that were frightening her had vanished one by one. Mani visited her as usual. The house was full of happiness. Megha remembered her father's image that brought misery and was puzzled about his appearance. But she did not have the courage to talk about him to her mom. Moreover she thought that she needed to forget those painful things in life.

It was a holiday due to a bandh called by the opposition parties against inflation. So Megha was at home, dusting and arranging the book shelf along with her mom. Bharathi had gone out to meet her friend who was just a few blocks away. It was eleven in the morning. The door bell beckoned Megha to the door. She was surprised to see an elderly couple. The lady asked, "Is it Bharathi's house?" Megha nodded. They said, "We are Suryakumar's parents. We had come to meet Bharathi." Megha called them in and asked them to sit. She called her mom. Megha gave them water to drink and waited for them to talk.

They said, "Suryakumar has said a lot about you all and Bharathi. We wanted to meet you all. We had come for a function in our relatives place. We took this opportunity to visit you. We are living in Bangalore. I have two sons and a daughter who are all well employed and in a very good position in the society. This son Surya, he never wants to listen to us. The service he does is good and I am proud. But he needs to settle in life. He has to work somewhere and earn too."

Suryakumar's father continued, with Megha and Vasundhara wondering, why on earth they were telling all these things to them. "We thought that bondage will bring a sense of responsibility in him. He refused to marry and avoided us, whenever we talked about marriage. We couldn't find a girl who could accept his principles. We asked him to go for a proper job and do service, when time let him do."

Megha wondered, if these people wanted her mom to advise Suryakumar and waited for them to continue, as they both were silent for a few seconds. Megha asked them if they wanted tea or coffee. But they asked Megha to wait till they finished telling them what they wanted to.

Surya's father said," We were surprised, when Surya kept talking about Bharathi for the past two months and we too were interested in knowing who the girl was. We came to know about her illness and the way she had recovered from Surya. Last week when he came to Bangalore, we told him to get married, as he was nearing 32. Usually he used to avoid or change the topic. But this time, he told us that he would marry, if the girl he wishes to marry agrees."

Surya's mom said, "What else do we need on this earth?. We were happy, but we were not sure, if the girl and her family would accept our wish. That's why we had come to ask Bharathi and you of your opinion about Suryakumar." They finished and waited for the response from Vasundhara. Surya's mom asked, "Where is Bharathi?"

Megha replied, She has gone to a friend's house. Shall I make tea for you both?". Megha prepared sugarless tea for them. She offered to them an apple cut into small pieces and a few biscuits in a plate with tea. She gave tea to her mom also. Her mom asked her to bring Bharathi from her friend's place. Megha told, "Aunty, I will bring Bharathi here." Megha wondered if Bharathi would accept this proposal. These people wanted the marriage soon. She was doubtful, if Bharathi would agree to that.

Megha told Bharathi, "You have an important visitor darling, so we have to go home, right now. "Bharathi tried in many ways to know who had come, by nagging Megha on their way back home. When she saw the couple, she did not know who they were. She stood curiously. They introduced themselves and she was surprised.

Bharathi folded her hands in respect and welcomed them. She looked curiously waiting to know the reason for their visit. They did not make her wait for long. They asked her, "What do you think of my son Surya, Bharathi?"

She said," Of course, he is a gem, aunty. I like him for his service mindedness. He told me what life was all about, when I was scared and depressed. He is amazing, aunty. I have seen the way he treats the mentally sick. He is so patient and very kind. There are not many people who understand or are supportive of these afflicted people. The service Suryakumar is doing is commendable." They all watched Bharathi, with a smile on their face, as she went on and on.

Surya's mom told her husband, "Finally we have found a girl who admires him. So I think I can ask her what we wanted to."

"Bharathi, will you marry Surya? ", the mother asked. Bharathi stood silent for some time and then asked them about Surya's opinion. Suryakumar's father said, "He wants to marry you. But he wants to know what you think about him." Bharathi smiled and turned to her mom and sister. Surya's mom said," Bharathi, you can take your time and tell us your opinion. You don't have to hurry, darling. My instincts tell me that we have found an apt match for him."

They both left happy, giving her their phone number. Vasundhara asked Bharathi to sit near her and asked her feebly, if she liked Surya and whether the marriage proposal was acceptable to her. Megha too told her sister that Surya was a nice person and she was sure that Bharathi would be happy with him.

Bharathi seemed to be immersed in thoughts. Bharathi called the hospital to know, if Suryakumar was there. He wasn't there. She left a message and waited for his call. Megha and her mom exchanged meaningful glances. She asked Megha, "What do you think Megha?". Megha said, "Bharathi, its your life. It is for you to decide. We know that Suryakumar is a nice person. He understands the pain of others. So he will not hurt you in anyway." Their mom wrote down, "Bharathi, I will be happy, if you accept Suryakumar. He is the best choice for you, as he was with you, during your difficult times too."

When Suryakumar called Bharathi, it was past three in the evening. Till then, Bharathi was restless. She told him," Surya, your parents had come to visit us." Suryakumar was surprised," Is it? They did not tell me, Bharathi. What did they say?" Bharathi smiled, when she told, "about your wish." Surya asked, "What wish?" He wanted Bharathi to spell out the things and Bharathi kept dodging.

Finally Surya said, "I wanted them to voice my wish. So, what did you say, Bharathi?" Bharathi dragged," you ask me the question, and then I will answer you. Otherwise, I will answer the people who asked me." There was silence for a few minutes, then Surya asked after a cough, "Will you be my life partner too, Bharathi, now that you are my business partner?"

Bharathi paused then said," Yes Sir, wish granted . . . ." and laughed. The four eyes that were watching the interaction expressed happiness and thanks to the Lord who made Bharathi bubbly and happy, as she was three years before. Bharathi and Surya talked for some time.

Megha was asked to convey Bharathi's consent to Surya's parents. Even before Megha could start, Surya's mom expressed her happiness. Surya had told them already. They also wanted the marriage to be a simple affair. Surya's mom said, "My sons and daughter will come to visit India in January. We can have their marriage then". They knew about Megha's marriage on 26th January. So they decided to have the marriage on the same date. Vasundhara wanted to know how they wished the marriage function to be. They were acceptable to a simple function in the registrar office. They also decided to have a banquet in Bangalore after a few days to introduce the couple.

At first both Bharathi and Suryakumar were against the idea of marriage before his dream hospital was completed, but they consented due to the pressure from Surya's side. Muthu and Nirmala were happy to know about the wedding of Bharathi. Muthu thanked her Goddess for the grace she had showered on them.

Muthu wanted the three girls to accompany her, when she fulfilled her vow by walking on fire. Megha was frightened to see people walking on fire, but Bharathi wanted to make Muthu happy. So they all decided to go with Muthu.

The temple was crowded. There was a long queue waiting to walk on fire. When Muthu's turn came, all the three felt the pain. They saw selfless Muthu close her eyes and walk praying for the well beings of the people she loved. They held their breath till she finished her walk.

When she came out of the fire walk, Megha inspected her foot. There were blisters, but Muthu was very happy. She did not mind it. They all worshipped the Goddess and returned home. The three girls cooked and served the food, allowing Muthu to take rest.

The beginning of December saw the light festival and then came the month of Markazhi, a month dedicated to the worship God. It is about Andal, an ardent devotee of Lord Vishnu. She fasted, sang and worshipped Lord Vishnu and got united with him. Even now, her songs called Thiruppavai is sung early in the morning during this month.

The New year started the countdown for the marriage of the three princesses. After Pongal, a week before the marriage, Muthu and Nirmala stayed in Megha's house. While Megha bought cotton sarees, Bharathi and Nirmala bought simple silk sarees for the occasion. As Megha was to live with her in laws, her in laws did not want her to bring any furniture or utensils. They said they had enough of everything from gold to dust and Megha need not bring anything with her.

Suryakumar lived in a flat near the hospital Ashraya. He had very few things. So Vasundhara furnished the house with basic things needed to run the household. Surya's parents too converted the bachelor's enclave into a liveable mansion. As for Nirmala, Ganesan took a small flat for rent in the city to enable Nirmala to commute easily. Nirmala and Ganesan furnished their dream house, while Vasundhara gifted them with things needed for the household. Nirmala's brother told Nirmala that he will gift her a scooty in his first month's salary. Ganesan made fun saying, "It looks like everyone is giving me dowry. I don't want anything. I can take care of my angel. I need nothing." He turned to Nirmala's brother, "my dear boy, give that money to me, we will use it to give treatment to the poor. I will get your sis a scooty right now." All was set for marriage. All of them waited eagerly for the day to arrive.

The day did arrive in all glamour and the three maidens got married. While Meghas, Nirmalas and Bharathis went to visit the orphanage, Muthu and Vasundhara returned home as they had to make arrangement for the dinner they were to host.

Bharathi came to her house with Surya's family, as they had planned to start for Bangalore two days after marriage. Vasundhara wanted to give a luncheon in her house for the brides and grooms the next day after wedding. Bharathi played the CD containing one of the lectures of her mom. Her in laws loved it so much, that they wanted listen to all her lectures. Megha and Nirmala were invited with their husbands and their families for a luncheon the day after the wedding. So Muthu was busy, preparing the dishes, along with Vasundhara. There were lot of helping hands too. The children were breathing life into the house with their pranks and talks. Megha arrived with Mani around ten in the morning. Nirmala came half an hour later.

Megha looked beautiful in her blue green cotton saree. Nirmala and Bharathi were in salwars. They had the glow of the brides on their faces which made them prettier. Bharathi's in laws and kids had gone to the temple nearby. Megha went to her favourite place, the window and sat in the chair. She saw mynahs' playing around. Then the golden bird, Bharadwaj came slowly and sat on the basin to drink water. It had shining plumes and a long tail. She slowly dipped her head to bathe. Megha turned to see, if

Mani was around. He was standing in a corner of the room, watching Megha. She asked him to come near her without making any sound. She showed the bird that was busy dipping itself and enjoying a refreshing bath. Bharathi who saw this called her mom, Muthu and Nirmala, who were in kitchen and showed them. Suryakumar and Ganesan too joined them. They all stood silently watching the couple.

Bharathi commented "Dear Dr. Subramanian, my sister will not leave the window or the chair. Those are her possessions. Do you have a window Sir, in your house where my sister can see tree pies, kingfishers and woodpeckers? Megha, take that chair with you, as it felt lonely without you yesterday, darling". Everyone laughed.

Muthu had seen this family in happiness, after initial struggles and problems, when the children were growing up. But that happiness had a small tinge of sadness or sorrow behind. This happiness was complete. Vasundhara had achieved the goal she had set for her, braving the troubles that came her way, showing the people who respected her and to her children that truth always triumphs in the end. She paved a path woven with ideals and morals and followed it showing people the very purpose of life.

Vasundhara eyed Muthu with pride. Muthu, a woman, who had nothing to call her own, but could still feel happy over the happiness and success of others. Life had not been a cake walk for both the women. Vasundhara slogged and endured all the problems that came her way to give her children the best. Muthu had slogged and tried to give all the support, she could give to see the happiness in the woman, who stood alone with the two small kids, after getting separated from her cruel husband.

TIDE 22

Vaundhara relaxed, after a hectic and lively week, listening to music. The noisy house of the earlier day was engulfed in silence. Megha and Nirmala had left the day before and Bharathi left with her in laws to Bangalore that morning. Muthu had stayed back to help Vasundhara and to see off Bharathi.

Muthu said, "the house looks very silent after all the celebrations. Are you feeling lonely ma?"

Vasundhara smiled and said "No"

She talked slowly and softly. She had started talking a few sentences, but in a very feeble tone. She went on, "Muthu, I am the happiest person on this earth. Why should I feel lonely? This loneliness is beautiful. A river keeps flowing in its course. When a log or wooden plank is set afloat, it sends it to the shore and doesn't claim its ownership. Neither does it cling to it. If the wood stays in the water, it will not be of any use. It will rot. Whereas, when it is sent to the shore, it will be useful to someone who needs it. Likewise, children are born to us. We need to teach them to be good and be confident and to live for and with a reason. We cannot hold them forever. They will rot. Now it is their duty to spread their branches and grow and ours is to watch them and enjoy." She coughed because of the strain of talking. Muthu got her water to drink.

After sometime she continued, "I am not going to work in the college, Muthu, as I have enough savings to maintain myself. I will go to the college occasionally, as honorary professor. I will give lectures after I get back my voice fully and visit the temples and places which I had always wanted to".

"Amma after my son gets a job, I will also come with you to all the places. Will you take me with you?"

"Of course Muthu, I will. But you still have responsibilities. So perform those well and then you can come with me."

TIDE 23

Life is always full of struggles. It is these struggles that make a person stronger and matured. A caterpillar undergoes struggles to transform itself into a chrysalis. It emerges as a beautiful butterfly after the pains it had to endure. Anyone can live a pedestrian life but living a meaningful life is important. Setting up goals and living an idealistic life is very difficult. One needs to face myriads of problems to continue being idealistic.

I have been watching Vasundhara's family right from the day she got married. She stuck to her principles, never compromising on anything for the sake of money or luxury. She was shattered, when her husband doubted her. Trust is the clasp that holds tight any relationship, be it marriage or friendship. When trust is broken, nothing stays. She started living for her kids. There are many single mothers in India like Muthu and Vasundhara. Vasundhara had an advantage as she was educated and well employed. Though her salary was not very high, she had a permanent income.

As for Muthu, she had no support even with her husband around, as he used to always drink with her hard earned and slept merrily, while she slogged for kids. When he left her, it came as a relief, as the money he stole was used for other purposes. Being uneducated, she did not know the priorities of life or value of education.

Life is full of surprises. I always expected that Megha will turn to service fully and Bharathi would be a person who will earn a lot and live a comfortable and romantic life.

But destiny had different plans for them. Megha became a person who had a romantic life with Dr. Subramanian. Though they were service minded, they did not devote themselves completely to it.

On the contrary, Bharathi turned out to be completely service minded who took only a meagre amount needed to survive. I had a doubt earlier whether death can bring change in a person's mindset. After seeing a few people myself, I believe it can. All human minds cannot be defined to follow the same orbit, like each planet has a different orbit. Hence the difference in the way each individual reacts to the same situation. I have seen people take up to philosophy after having a tryst with death. Some opt to end their lives as a solution to the sorrows, while some become a theist.

When Bharathi saw the accident, the death and an orphaned child in a spur of a moment, something made her stop and think. She got a lesson that the money or luxury she thought was ultimate cannot buy life or stop death. She was shocked by the realisation of what life really was. The spark made her depressed, dejected and an escapist but later moulded her into a better individual and taught her the purpose of birth and the reason to live.

The character, Nirmala is actually a representative of many girls in the villages who are killed for being a girl. Female infanticide still exists in this all parts of our country.I was shocked when I read a few months in the daily 'The Hindu' about an Indian woman who was a doctor.She decided to kill her child in the womb when she found out it was a female in her scan.

I never thought Nirmala will soar to such heights with all the hardships she had to endure. Had she been killed, when she was born Muthu's lifestyle wouldn't have improved. She made her family proud. It's true that if a girl is given education, the whole family is enlightened and generations can taste the fruit of education. She did not forget the ladder she used for climbing neither the state she was in. So she started a trust along with her life partner Dr.Ganesan to help girls who were intelligent but couldn't afford an education

Muthu having realised her folly now advices her friends to educate girls. True to say, Nirmala ended up in good hands that are Vasundhara's. Not all are that lucky. There aren't many in this world who are willing to help others, when they themselves are in despair. In this land where the country and rivers are seen as mother, it is sad to know that girls are unwanted.

Vasundhara, a strong believer of destiny believed that no one can stop something from happening. But she doesn't mean inaction or laziness is good. Her philosophy is, if we do our duty, we are good and honest; whatever we deserve will reach us. Truth and dharma always triumphs in the end. Suryakumar, Shivashankar and Ganesan are people who are very rare to be seen. Not many can throw the comforts that money offers and live selflessly. It is these people who make the earth a very good place to live in by setting good examples.

As for Vasudevan, Vasundhara's husband . . . . I was also curious like you all, to know what had befallen him. I enquired one of his friends who lives in Mumbai. His life took a different course after he separated from Vasundhara. The girl he married was timid with no one to support her. As she had nowhere to go, she stayed with him patiently. They had two sons who hated their father for his arrogance and his attitude towards their mom. The boys studied well and settled abroad not wanting to even see his shadow after their mother's death.

When he blackmailed them with his property, they declined all their rights towards the property of their father. Vasudevan who thought that money can buy anything and hold everyone to him was shocked. He was already addicted to drugs and alcohol. The fall was too much that he got more addicted. He lost all his wealth.

Hearing this, one of the sons wanted to put him in a de-addiction center which he did forcibly. He escaped from the centre where he was admitted and my guess is—thats when he landed in Megha's place dirty and shabby.

My friend told me that a few months back he received a call from a girl who said she had found my friend's visiting card in the pocket of a man. From the description she gave he guessed that it was Vasudevan. She said that he was found unconscious on the sidewalk. The friend had given details of him.When she said that she had called from Chennai, my friend had told that he had a wife by name Vasundhara. When he enquired about her, she said that her name was Bharathi. She gave the number of a hospital where Vasudevan was admitted to be conveyed to his sons.

When I talked to Bharathi, I came to know that she sympathised with her father which was also surprising to me as I really saw an ocean of change in her attitude. She told Suryakumar about him. They both admitted him in a hospital. After he got better, he was put in a home where he stays. He now repents for the sins he had done. I think there will come a day, when Bharathi will reveal her identity to him for she said she hadn't.

Bharathi decided not to tell her mom about this but told Megha who couldn't bring herself to see him There is a famous thirukural in Tamil,

'Inna seidharai oruthal avar nana nannayam seiydhu vidal' . . . which means, we should do good to the person who had done bad things to us making him ashamed of his deeds . . . .

So life keeps moving waiting for none. There are tides in everybody's life. There isn't an ocean without tides but in the midst stands an island that looks so beautiful . . . . Life is beautiful with its struggles, strives and difficulties. Love looks beautiful, when given to a person who needs it the most than craving for love.

Life is beautiful and glorious

After the tides of sorrows subside

Just like the radiance that looks beautiful

As the dark gloomy clouds reveal the sun . . . .